I0582573

The Pilgrim's Journey: Flashes of Awakening

Copyright © 2022 Robert H. Wellington III

This book is a work of fiction and reflects thoughts, ideas and theories of the author.

All rights reserved. No part of this book may be reproduced, distributed, or transmitted in any form or by any means, including photocopying, recording, or other electronic or mechanical methods, without prior written permission from the publisher or author, except in the case of brief quotations embodied in critical reviews and certain other noncommercial uses permitted by copyright law.

ISBN

Paperback	978-1-68547-213-9
Hardcover	978-1-68547-214-6
eBook	978-1-68547-215-3

Library of Congress Control Number: 2023900722

Printed in the United States of America

FRISCO, TX 75034
United States
www.wa-publishing.com

THE
PILGRIM'S
JOURNEY

FLASHES *of* AWAKENING

ROBERT H. WELLINGTON III

TABLE OF CONTENTS

INTRODUCTION   XIII

FORWARD   XV

Chapter 1: Whispers Across Time and Space   1

    The Pilgrims Journey – A Ballad   2

Chapter 2: A Pilgrim in Hiding   13

Chapter 3: The Pilgrim's Song   17

    The Sacred Hologram   17

Chapter 4: The Pilgrim Awakens   25

Chapter 5: Meditation   27

    Touching the Higher Realms   27

Chapter 6: A Few Flashes of Awakening   35

Chapter 7: Some Thoughts On Love   41

    Love's Song   42

    Blending With Love   44

Chapter 8: More Flashes   47

    The Lie   47

    The Call and the Answer   49

    Family Solidarity   50

    Earth – Our Home   51

Chapter 9: Beyond   53

    Reclaimed Salvation   53

Chapter 10: Escape from the Dream   55

Chapter 11: Pilgrim Missteps   57

Chapter 12: All He Made, That Thou Art   59

Chapter 13: Creation   61

Chapter 14: Both Flower and Thorn   63

Chapter 15: The Purpose of Life   65

Chapter 16: New Life   67

        A Baby is Born   67

Chapter 17: A Parents Song for Their Teenager   69

Chapter 18: Crossing Over   71

        A Good Man Moves On   71

        A Life Well Lived   73

        To A Loving Mother   75

        Goodbye Dear Friend   77

        Moving On   79

Chapter 19: Musings on Vibration   81

Chapter 20: Musings on Particles and Waves   83

Chapter 21: The Call of Stillness   85

Chapter 22: Food For Thought   87

        Become the Teacher   87

        See Yourself in Everything and Everything in Yourself   88

        Infinite Consciousness   88

Chapter 23: A Loving Sign Post   91

        Won't You Be Mine   92

Chapter 24: The Pilgrim and The Threshold   95

Chapter 25: Some Thoughts on Depression   97

Chapter 26: To the Lost Ones   99

        A Parent's Lament   99

        To A Friend Who Is Lost   101

Chapter 27: A Tough Letter of Love   105

Chapter 28: Service   111

        Sharing One's Light   111

Chapter 29: To Those That Will Love Us Forever   113

        To The Mothers   113

        A Father's Strength   116

Chapter 30: Some Musings On Time   119

Chapter 31: Excerpts From Letters to A Loved One during Recovery   **125**

     Letter 1   125

     Letter 2   127

     Letter 3   127

     Letter 4   130

     Letter 5   131

     Letter 6   132

     Letter 7   134

     Letter 8   136

     Letter 9   138

     Letter 10   140

Chapter 32: Still More Flashes   **143**

     Who Am I   143

     The Realm of Silence   144

Chapter 33: Finding One's Joy   **145**

Chapter 34: Transcending Pain   **149**

     For I Am Here   150

Chapter 35: A Father's Prayer for A Lost Loved One   **153**

     Lost   154

Chapter 36: A Dialog With Perfection   **157**

Chapter 37: Love - Our Life Blood   **159**

     So What Is Love?   159

Chapter 38: The Ultimate Objective   **163**

     Two Become One   163

Chapter 39: Reach Higher   **165**

Chapter 40: A Few Closing Thoughts   **169**

     Duality   169

     Wholeness   169

     The Continuum   170

Chapter 41: A Poem in Closing   **171**

     Spirit's Call   172

     Our Divine Partnership   172

EPILOGUE   **175**

INTRODUCTION

We all are on a great journey, the Pilgrims Journey home. This is a journey with many paths, but one destination, the sacred feet of the One consciousness behind all.

This book is one such path, a path discovered in meditation and followed through love. It is one way of looking at the world and penetrating the fog of worldly illusion. Some might see it as a start, others as encouragement to continue. But in truth, all of us have been on the journey home, the journey of the Prodigal Sons and Daughters, since the beginning of time.

Although each pathway home is unique to each traveling pilgrim, there are many signposts, along the way, that are common to all. These include the call from within, hearing the call, reflections from the silence, flashes of awakening, messages of love, virtuous living, ripples in time and service to others. As we take each step forward we are also confronted with challenges, illusions, false guides, temptations and related missteps. Correct choices guided by loving service and faith are the keys to moving through and past these karmic delays and into His holy light.

This book attempts to remind the reader of some of these markers; sign posts known to all, but temporarily obscured by worldly illusion. These words hope to bring a reflection of their energy into the world, a reminder of our intimate connectedness and common purpose. We all have access to their magic. We have only to quiet the mind and listen. These sign posts reveal themselves in meditation, contemplation, insight and intuition. Their energy is shared through artistic expression, compassionate understanding and selfless service.

Through poetry and prose the author has tried to bring these ideas into the physical world. I apologize in advance for only capturing a small piece of their essence, but if the reader connects through his or her heart, perhaps they will feel the same loving energy trying so desperately to break through the density of the 3D world. When something loving moves us deep within, then we are on the right track. Let your heart be your guide, your mind be the servant and partner of the heart, and you will never stray far from the path.

General Comment;

The Pilgrim's Journey is the story of each of us, male and female. Please understand that the Pilgrim is not gender specific. Accordingly, read each him as him/her, etc.

FORWARD

All is alive and vibrating. God began the cycle of creation with the perfect harmony of His Word. One word and all that exists or will exist came into being. Yes, even the future came into being, separated only by the illusion of time. All that is seen, all that is unseen, all ideas, and all knowledge came into being with His word. That which seemingly remains undiscovered waits only for conscious intent to touch it and know its truth.

Many awakened ones have touched these truths and brought their beauty down to us that we might glimpse God through their gifts of creativity, writings, art, scientific advances and infinite inspirational sharing's. These are gifts of Love. Love comes in many forms, shapes and sizes, The artist gives his or her love through their art, the poet through his or her writing; The true friend through his or her kindness, generosity, patience, compassion, willingness to forgive and understanding.

Through direct experience or subtle symbolism, the pilgrim

discovers and leaves signs for all of us who follow. They are like blazes marking a forest trail, guiding each of us, until the day that our powers of concentration and contemplation can know these mysteries directly.

CHAPTER 1

WHISPERS ACROSS TIME AND SPACE

We are all Prodigal Sons and Daughters somewhere in time and space. We are all on the pilgrim's journey home. For millennia we journeyed into ever increasing levels of density, sent from the One consciousness behind and within all. After long eons, the miracle of His song penetrated the darkness and we stopped our downward descent. Did His song penetrate to our level or did we evolve the sensitivity to hear it and begin to recognize it?

The seemingly endless search for awakening and enlightenment **is** the Pilgrim's Journey. We are all on it, to one degree or another. Some are actively pursuing it, and in so doing, consciously assisting with the establishment of His Kingdom on Earth. Many have turned an ear towards its call, wondering at the distant recognition of its familiar symphonic alure, but not yet ready to follow it. A few do their best to ignore or hide from it, for fear of confrontation with the Divine, and many are still fast asleep.

God's song, always and forever, is available to all who have found sufficient inner peace to hear it and then choose to follow it. All were sent out or, in the author's opinion, chose to enter this world and experience whatever creation had to offer. The first part of the path, the path of *involution* is the journey from pure spirit into ever increasing density. The *evolutionary* path begins with the turn homeward and ends with the realization, or more correctly, the remembrance, of our oneness with the Father.

The Ballad which follows is the story of "The Pilgrim's Journey." It is the story of the men and women who have heard the call and are overwhelmed by a desire to find its source and melt into its perfection. It is also the story of the evolution of his/her awakening wisdom as the journey is relentlessly pursued and illuminated by ever increasing levels of understanding, ever brighter *Flashes of Awakening.*

The Pilgrims Journey – A Ballad

Refrain:
Searching far and wide for treasure
Chasing all on earth that shines
Diamonds, gems and earthly pleasures
He was lost among the vines
Endless hunger burns within him
From the pain, he seeks release
Till the guide inside reminds him
Search the heart to find true peace

What here follows is a story,
Of a man who traveled far.
This a story with a message,

Offered as a guiding star.

Message herein for the searchers.

Those who hear the sacred song.

Those who long to find the treasure,

Awakening from sleep so long.

Hear the song of endless calling.

Calling to the children lost

Calling with healing forgiveness.

Find it, no matter the cost.

Mystery, the sacred music,

Must be solved to wake from sleep.

Oh, his heart longs for the secret.

Must reach out, to those that weep.

Maybe truth's around the corner.

Maybe riches, maybe power.

Maybe a new gem that sparkles.

He must find it, now's the hour.

Maybe chasing all that's shiny.

Maybe that's the answer sought.

He will press on and soon conquer,

All that binds him, every knot.

For his earthly will is powerful.

Focused mind should soon achieve.

He will press on, nothing stops him.

He will win the prize he seeks.

Decades pass and he's successful,

At obtaining worldly wealth.

Wealthy beyond his consumption.

Wealth that only leads to death.

And his heart still feels so empty.

Has he led himself astray?

Has he wasted precious moments?

Is this one big masquerade?

And from deep within a murmur.

Faintly heard through aching heart.

Child, your longing's misdirected,

Chasing all that shines on earth.

This a recipe for sadness.

Which can never fill the void.

You're a child of Love's perfection.

Manifested love and joy.

Answers lie within your being.

Look within to find the truth.

You reside within the infinite.

Not the matrix, you call earth.

For a moment, he could feel it.

Loving wisdom filling him.

It was just a flash in silence.

In that flash, a holy hymn.

Refrain:

Searching far and wide for treasure

Chasing all on earth that shines

Diamonds, gems and earthly pleasures

He was lost among the vines

Endless hunger burns within him

From the pain he seeks release

Till the guide inside reminds him

Search the heart to find true peace

Just a flash, but something touched him,

Well beyond his earthly life.

Images from silent knowing.

Sacred path past earthly strife.

Where to look, he starts to ponder.

How to find that healing light.

Longs to feel that warm completeness.

Longs to make his mis-steps right.

So, he searched with endless effort,

Endless research, endless leads.

Answers just around the corner.

Prepare the earth and plant the seeds

Endlessly, acquired knowledge,

Books and writings, he absorbed.

But his heart ached in the silence.

Nothing seemed to fill the void.

Knowledge too, was a possession.

Just more things, which weighed him down.

Maybe this is not the answer.

Maybe this is not the crown?

Perhaps wise ones could direct him.

Perhaps a guru or a preacher.

Surely, they will have the answer.

Surely one could be his teacher.

So, in search, again he traveled.

He crossed the path of many wise.

Many that were false, misleading.

Very few could open eyes.

Then one rose above the others.

Looking kindly on the man.

With a look of knowing, uttered.

Look inside for sacred land.

No one in your steps can travel.

Only you can walk your road.

Each of us uniquely journeys,

At your birth was this bestowed.

Listen to your heart which calls you.

Know it as your very own.

Feel the bliss and know with confidence,

You are on the pathway home.

No one else but you can find it.
Each uniquely knows the way.
Follow love inside which guides you.
Through your love turn night to day.

With these words the teacher left him.
With a tear, he turned to say.
Love inside will never fail you.
Inward journey is the way.

All alone he sat and pondered.
Oh, so close and yet so far.
Sitting there, the Silence saw him.
Soon dispelling his despair.

Comforting, it whispered softly.
Look within and I will share.
With internal contemplation,
You will find the golden stair.

In the Silence, he found loving,
Thoughts of family and of friends.
Thoughts connecting, all existing.
Filling all the voids within.

Healing wounds, so long he carried.
False companions, held so dear.
Now were gone, replaced by Silence.
On his cheek a lonely tear.

Refrain:

Searching far and wide for treasure

Chasing all on earth that shines

Diamonds, gems and earthly pleasures

He was lost among the vines

Endless hunger burns within him

From the pain he seeks release

Till the guide inside reminds him

Search the heart to find true peace

Peace beyond all comprehension.

All potential within reach.

New acceptance and forgiveness,

Replaying the wise one's speech.

Had he found that something special?

Had he found the chalice lost?

Sitting there his eyes now opened.

With new vision now, he saw.

So much clarity and knowing.

So much love had set him free.

He sat there for countless moments.

Restless mind, now quiet sea.

Thoughts of family soon awoke him.

Once was shackled, now he's free.

Must serve all, in joy's communion.

Serving is the sacred key.

Finding love within he traveled,
Near and far to share the word.
Awakening that something special.
In all met upon the road.

Knowing now the truth's within him.
Veiled until love's inflamed.
Love that's shared without an effort.
Love once lost but now reclaimed.

Those encountered, feel that special,
Energy that's from the All.
Energy that Love inspires.
Resurrecting those that fall.

The true healer knows the secret.
He's the instrument, not the cure.
Choosing to let God flow through him.
Healing all and making pure.

We are vessels for His glory.
Yet He longs for us to know.
Our true kinship as His body.
Sacred oneness with God's flow.

With that thought wisdom awakens.
Blindness now is perfect sight.
Knowing truth resides within him,
In his heart he holds it tight.

Though the ego begs to differ.
Working hard to claim its place.
"I was there when you were single."
"I was there to be your face."

But the light of truth shines on it.
Yes, my friend you played a roll.
Now let go and be a witness.
To the truth that makes one whole.

In the light, the ego softened.
For it too began to see.
All we meet upon the journey.
Play a part in Love's great play.

Slowly fading from existence.
Knowing that it played its role.
Farewell to an old companion,
Diamond now where once was coal.

So, the truth does not reside in,
Things that do not dwell within.
Neither guru's, will, nor treasures,
Can the emptiness, they fill.

This he gives to those that follow.
Stepping through the curtain tear.
Use it as you will my family.
It is here for all to share

Refrain:

Searching far and wide for treasure

Chasing all on earth that shines

Diamonds, gems and earthly pleasures

He was lost among the vines

Endless hunger burns within him

From the pain he seeks release

Till the guide inside reminds him

Search the heart to find true peace

CHAPTER 2

Some hear the call and desperately try to follow the still small voice within, as in the poem, "A Pilgrim's Journey." Some Pilgrims, however, run from the call for fear that his or her missteps will evoke Divine punishment. This thinking, separate from the Divine Principle, is soon dispelled, for upon awakening, all find they are healed by His perfect forgiveness.

A Pilgrim in Hiding

> With eyes downcast, avoiding stares,
> He runs and hides with focused care.
> From age to age and life to life,
> Avoiding service and the light.
>
> He is confused, he lives in fear,
> Of waking up and seeing clear,
> The truth he thinks so terror filled,

Of past mistakes, earth left untilled.
He feels safe with eyes closed tight.
He hides in blindness without sight.
For there, it's safe, no one to see.
His silent prayer, please don't judge me.

For I have run when you have called,
Shrunk when others have stood tall
For I'm not worthy and I dread
Confronting paths I should have tread.

I run now from your burning gaze.
I hide in shadows and the haze.
In hope you'll lose all sight of me.
Why take a chance when unworthy?

And now I quiver in the cold.
 My soul's of lead and not of gold.
I'm safe and hidden out of view.
No chance of being found by you.

And in the darkness there he hides,
So far from where the light abides.
Or so he thought as eons went.
Unworthy still, his life force spent.

He felt so empty, all alone.
Yet deep inside he dreamed of home.
He thought, how could life be so cold.
There must be more if dreams unfold.

Do I dare venture from this cave?
Will He see me and soon enslave?
Is such a fate worse than this dark,
This nothingness, this realm so stark?

Such thoughts of home, I need to know.
Will I be chained, if choose to go?
Yet something deep, it spurred him on.
He left the dark to find the dawn.

He'll face the scorn of his accusers.
Face the lash of his abusers.
He prays his verdict will be swift.
His life is over, end it quick.

He falls to knees upon the ground.
He feels a light, intense, profound.
It penetrates his very being.
A weight is lifted, oh such healing.

Silently he hears a song.
Familiar tones, but gone so long.
His body glows with new vibration.
He sees himself, one with creation.

He feels a peace, there is no fright.
His very being turns to light.
His body like a feather floats,
Past barriers and over moats.

Which he had built, his mis-creation.
Fading now to hearts elation.
He hears a symphony and other,
Voices welcoming their brother.

And light so brilliant, deep within.
He feels awakening begin.
And as he looks oer God's domain,
He sees a void that bears his name.

For only he can fill this span,
Prepared for him when time began.
He gently floats and takes his place
To thunderous cheers, love lights his face

For he was certain of defeat.
Yet with I Am, he takes a seat.
He now is one within the flow,
The tapestry complete and whole.

CHAPTER 3

THE PILGRIM'S SONG

So, what is the call; this song which is so irresistible to each of us on the Pilgrims Journey? Where does it emanate from? What is its cause?

I wrote the following essay, "The Sacred Hologram" several decades ago in an attempt to answer these questions and others related to creation and evolution, both physical and spiritual. It is not a proven scientific theory. It is only my heart felt hypothesis: Musings presented to my readers so they can come to their own conclusions. It is a discussion of Light and Love and the miracle they play in the powerful interaction of creation and evolution.

This discussion on the Sacred Hologram can also be found within Chapter 9 of my book, **Water Wisdom**, *Part One, A Journey of Discovery*.

THE SACRED HOLOGRAM

The concepts of Creation and Evolution currently reside in

separate and distinct theories. The sponsors of each theory see little commonality with the other. My proposal comes from a spiritual perspective. It relates scientific principals in a unique way, but has not been fully vetted by the scientific method. I present it for those with an open mind as an alternative; an alternative that brings the competing theories together in a cohesive working relationship.

If nothing else it is food for thought. In my view, each of these competing points of view has its role to play. Creation and evolution are intimately related and should not stand in sharp contrast to one another. Rather, they are two sides of the same coin. But, of course, it is not my view which is critical here. It is your viewpoint. Perhaps this new way of looking at these old adversaries can be a springboard to a new approach, breakthrough or paradigm.

I ask only that the reader keep an open mind as I present my thinking. If the words ring true, the rest will take care of itself.

LIGHT:

The photon has been shown to be an extremely efficient carrier of information as evidenced by the millions of miles of fiber optic cable crisscrossing the planet. I submit that imprinted within light's essence is all knowledge without exception. Who knows what secrets it may hold which we are currently unaware of. One might postulate that light (visible and invisible) is the carrier of God's incarnated message of truth.

Likewise, in a very real way God imprinted His message, the key to establishing heaven on earth, in each of our hearts and all of creation. This message is indelibly imprinted on everything that exists, from the largest star to the smallest subatomic particle.

The Hologram:

A hologram is a picture in a photographic medium (usually glass or plastic) made by light (in most cases a high-intensity laser). In a way, it is light crystallized in a photographic medium.

In simplified terms, a hologram is made by shining a laser on the subject to be photographed and splitting the light in such a way that one beam reaches the photographic medium slightly later and out of phase with the other split beam. Because the two beams or waves are out of phase when they come together, they have increased energy and excite the medium's atoms. The result: a 3D picture of the subject.

Sadly, directed energy weapons operate on a similar principal of interference. Interestingly this was also the principal of the Death Star in the movie "Star Wars," with which we are all so familiar. But I digress.

This is remarkable in and of itself, but the real mystery is that if you break the medium which holds the hologram, shattering it into many pieces, there is a perfect replica of the original 3D picture within each and every piece. The picture within each is not a fragment of the original picture but a complete copy. Think about that for a second.

It is a fractal, infinitely compressible. And if light is fractal and a constant between all that exists, then one might propose that the created world must also be fractal."

Interestingly, the larger pieces require less light to see the picture, but with varying intensities of light, each piece holds a true copy, no matter the size. If you could seamlessly reassemble several pieces, the original image becomes clearer and clearer with the amount of light required to view it varying inversely with the size. So a small fragment requires a greater intensity of light to view the image while a larger fragment, less so.

But what has this to do with creation, you ask? Well, here is one way to look at it that might help you understand what I am trying to convey.

If God is light (or at least light is the closest thing we know to God in the manifested universe) then at creation, during the Big Bang, Vishnu's dream, or other act of genesis, when unbelievable energy intensities exploded into the emptiness that became space-time; God's image, His truth, and His word was imprinted onto every atom and subatomic particle created, exactly like the hologram we just described. This ultimately expanded into what we today call the universe. Think about it, God's image imprinted on everything that exists from the smallest subatomic particle to the largest star.

What was the message that spirit imprinted? It has been called many things, but the simplest and most easily understood is *love.* Think about it—love is the ultimate message of the one consciousness. Being one with itself, it must attract itself. Imagine a created universe with its trillions and trillions and trillions of particles, each with God's message on it. Each particle must have a natural affinity for every other particle because love must attract itself. Throughout the ages each particle of star stuff with His image imprinted therein has had a natural affinity to organize itself with other star stuff into ever-increasing expressions of His truth and through ever-more-sophisticated forms—from the heavier elements created in the furnaces of the infinite stars to atoms combining into molecules, followed by single and then multi-cell organisms, then more complex organisms right up to man himself with his conscious ability to relate to his environment and ultimately to the cause behind it. Always the ocean of God's creation has longed to re-assemble the sacred hologram. Each new form expresses Source more and more completely until they reassembled into forms sophisticated enough to reconnect with consciousness and ultimately know the Father.

The consciousness within the imprinted message was and is the driving force behind the evolution to reassemble the sacred hologram. It wasn't survival of the fittest or natural selection that was behind evolution, it was consciousness calling to its own; imprinted on all that exists from the beginning of time

The more pieces of the sacred hologram that are organized together the louder spirit's song and the easier to experience it. The universe is, in a very real way, conscious of its creator and is thus able, in the silence, to know Him, their relationship to Him, and thus their true relationship to all. This conscious affinity (which many call love) is Source (for lack of a better term) striving throughout the ages to know It's creations, which are a part of Him, just as His creations have steadily evolved with seeming conscious evolutionary intent to know the Creator.

Think about the four forces of nature, gravity, electromagnetism, the strong force, and the weak force. I submit to you that all of these are manifestations of love. Scientists have searched for decades for the one unified force, when it has been right in front of them. It is love. Too often the obvious is ignored, especially by the scientific mind.

But things are changing in science. Higher physics and abstract spiritual concepts can hardly be distinguished from each other these days. In fact, the only way one can tell the difference is to look at who is saying them, scientist or philosopher. It is a wonderful thing to observe. Spirit's plan moves forward and will not be denied.

I'm sure these words sound confusing since the medium of language is so woefully deficient in explaining these concepts of essence. Perhaps if I explain it this way.

The one constant within the manifested universe is light or if you wish, energy or vibration. It is God incarnate, that which created all, giving each His word and the ability to choose. Choosing Him and the ultimate reassembly of His sacred hologram is the opportunity before us. He is the one constant.

We are here to learn to know Him, to realize that we are of Him and as such are not these bodies but something luminous, something reflective of His essence. Thus the universe's natural affinity for itself is in a very real way the expression of love. One might say that the prodigal children of His seed were sent out into nothingness (via the big bang or other act of beginning) to learn who they really are and in so doing, bring spirit's light to the lowest levels of incarnation and establish heaven on earth.

Ultimately all return to the Father, after long eons of choices, choices that ultimately transform into wisdom and from wisdom into a perfect image of the Father Himself, until one day one of our own was able to say, 'I and the Father are One.' This is the quest before each of us.

Words cannot adequately express any of God's mysteries. They exist in the realm of pure knowing. Ultimately the 3D world is about life and the forms through which the soul experiences it. Perhaps a few words in this area will be helpful.

Life is everywhere and in all things. When the One Cause said the word, it set in motion a vibration out of which creation emerged. From the stillness creation began and continues even today. This vibration is in all things and is the will behind all. From planetary rotation to the movement of subatomic particles, His vibration gives all life. From life's cycles to individual heartbeats, His vibration is the cause and the result of all that exists, seen and unseen. Thus we are intimately tied to the Father and each other.

All life has a natural affinity for itself, for it all came from the same Source. Truly we have the same Father from the smallest quark to man, arguably the most sophisticated life form on earth (although there are other sophisticated forms), a life form that is a symphony of many smaller parts. We have one Source, one song that vibrates through every atom. In that song are infinite octaves and harmonics, constantly expressing God through the infinite fractal of life. We are all brothers and sisters. We are made up of many parts, which come together by this natural affinity of attraction that is His will.

As life forms became more complex and sophisticated, a marvelous thing happened; consciousness was realized. Of course consciousness was always present, but we were unable to know it in this world until form, obeying this natural law of attraction, reached a sufficient level of sophistication and sensitivity. Again, this natural affinity we know in a higher sense as love.

Love draws together, which enables consciousness to know itself. One could say that it is this longing to know itself that is the essence of love. God longs to know Himself, just as we long to know God. Love is attracted to love. Beginning with the word, through the chaos of the beginning of time, to the organization of chaos (by virtue of His will and the energy of His spirit, which we call love), we have entered into consciousness, which has as its highest goal self-awareness. Standing on the summit of self-awareness, we know the Father and the Father knows Himself, for both are one. His kingdom has come. The prodigal son has returned home, and God who is infinite has become even greater. It is a great mystery.

CHAPTER 4

THE PILGRIM AWAKENS

And so it is time. The clock tower has struck. The hour has arrived. The time for holding back has past. The one who has slept so long, must now awaken. The world awaits as the vast man within, stretches his arms overhead and rubbing his eyes, greets the loving rays of an old friend, a friend long forgotten, his true Self.

Embracing the light the pilgrims body shudders as intense loving energy reinvigorates every atom within his or her waking body. Tears well up in the pilgrims eyes as they behold that which was long forgotten, the realm of pure Love, his home, the reality behind the form, Truth.

A balanced and perfect energy shoots up the spine. His head feels like it might explode as it tries to embrace the totality of creation. All are his family. With one pointed focus, the gates at the center of the forehead open and all is instantly revealed. All ancient blockages are cleared by the fires of truth, all illusions vaporized. Love flows through him without limit, blessing all within his awakened infinite view. His very essence has become pure embracing Love, expressed through selfless service, compassion, beauty, truth and wisdom.

And so creation moves to a new level, a higher level on the endless road back to the Father.

And so it is time.

And so it has begun.

-

CHAPTER 5

MEDITATION
Touching the Higher Realms

There are many ways for us to connect with the Call of His heavenly song. Each Pilgrim will find his or her unique approach. One proven approach, however, is meditation.

There are many excellent books on meditation and there are many approaches to its practice. Basically its objective is the quieting of the mind. It is simple to practice, but can be difficult to master. It's gifts are available to all with a little perseverance, but results are often hindered by a lack of consistency. Like exercising a muscle, meditation must be consistently practiced to achieve, maintain and intensify the tone and temper of one's mind.

The human mind through meditation and other spiritual practices is capable of touching revelation and in so doing touching the One mind. Sounds like a quest worth undertaking doesn't it? Unfortunately, such good intentions often fall victim to an unruly mind. I like to think of the brain as an exquisite antenna which can tune in to any subject that it is focused on. And indeed it can, but almost always this focus is disrupted by a lack of concentration, and the thousands of ideas and thought forms floating in the ether.

Do not be discouraged, however. The lower mind can be trained just like a muscle, **and it will get stronger.** The secret is perseverance and consistency.

There are many paths to God, and many ways to meditate. This short essay is a summary of what I found to work for me over 40 years, or so, of practice. I urge you to find your own way or ways. Whatever that regimen is, however, it will probably include some form of meditation.

I know this sounds daunting. You may be asking yourself, "How can I possibly practice steadily for one month, much less 40 years?"

The answer is that the benefits of meditation begin to be a significant contributing factor to an increasingly joyful and productive life, almost immediately. So whenever you start and for whatever length of time you are able to practice, the benefits are worth the effort. Think of it as exercise and training. We may not all become decathlon champions, but we all feel invigorated after a workout. Meditation is no different. Some will achieve Samadhi or a deep contemplative connection with the One, but all are taking a step closer to pure spirit with each effort.

Meditation is not in and of itself the goal. It can be a means to your spiritual objectives, but serving God, your Higher Power, the One pure Love, is the true objective. Begin your daily meditation with a deep knowing that your meditation serves that which is greater, whatever the name, although for the purposes of this discussion, I will most often use the term God. Every kindness, every unselfish act, every loving thought serves the greater and with it ever increasing illumination on the earthly plane.

"Thy kingdom come, thy will be done on earth as it is in heaven."

Sound familiar? Giving with loving intent is step one. Giving starts the flow of Love, like starting the flow of electricity by turning on a switch. Meditation is a pathway to God. God is Love, and so meditation must start with loving intent and selfless service without expectation of reward. Reward from the sharing of Love energy always comes, but the objective is giving. Let receiving take care of itself, for it is His law and must always flow to those who freely give.

LET'S BEGIN

If you are going to meditate, find a quiet place, a sacred place within your home, your place of worship, or favorite natural setting where you won't be disturbed. Find a comfortable place to sit. Whether you sit in a chair, cross legged or lotus position does not matter, but sitting with a straight back does. Slump and you will lose concentration or even fall asleep. A straight back allows the energy to flow up and down your spine, which in time will increasingly open the energy centers which we have come to know as the chakras. Energy is always flowing around the spine via the ida and pingala (Sanskrit terms) which circle the spine and its central channel, the sushumna (another Sanskrit word), in opposite spiraling directions.

This spiraling around the spine is also depicted in Hermes' staff, the Caduceus which we see in many medical establishments as a staff with two snakes wrapped around it in opposite directions and two wings at the top on either side.

When samadhi or deep contemplation is achieved the serpent fire coiled at the base of the spine, or kundalini (Sanskrit word meaning coiled serpent), shoots up through the sushumna, igniting all the chakras and illuminating the 1000 petal lotus at the crown of the head. This is the ultimate prize of spiritual pursuits and practices on earth, in my opinion. This is often referred to as a visit by the Holy Spirit, or a kundalini or chi awakening. Many who meditate regularly have experienced this to varying degrees. If it happens to you , you will know it. Remember, uniting with God is the quest. Having a kundalini experience is not. It may be a part of your journey, or it may not, but the benefits of regular meditation practice will always be a part of your experience and will always guide you in the right direction.

CONCENTRATION

So let's begin with concentration. Concentration is the quieting of the mind from its chronic attention deficit disorder (ADD) challenges. There are several ways that have been used over the eons to quiet the mind. Focusing on the breath, a seed thought, mantra, just sitting etc., are all tried and true approaches. My favorite is 'Meditation with seed.' This essentially is intensely focusing on a single seed thought, item, prayer, mantra, etc. Some people chant, or sing Amen or Om. It is not important. Quieting the mind is. As you sit, focus with one pointed concentration on your seed thought, prayer, or mantra, whatever you have chosen. Evaluate it as to form, its quality, its purpose and the cause behind it, whatever helps you to maintain a quiet mind and focus. You will find, almost immediately, that your focus has jumped from your seed thought to the ever flowing stream of consciousness that we know as the human mind.

For Example:

> *Johnny has soccer practice today. I better get him there early*
> *so he can practice his corner kicks. That reminds me, I need to*
> *pick up broccoli at the corner grocery after practice. Last time*
> *I was there I saw Jenny. She wanted to get together for dinner.*

The stream is endless. That is what the human mind does. It compares and relates endlessly. When you suddenly notice that your mind has taken you far away from the original seed thought, gently tell it to return to your meditation. Do not scold it, but rather tell it you love it and that it has been a faithful servant, but now it must refocus. For a minute or two it will quiet down, and then some other ADD trigger, a sound, a feeling, the phone ringing, will send the lower mind on another adventure of comparing and relating. When you notice that you, once again, have strayed from your seed thought, gently bring your mind back to focus. You will have to do this several times during the course of your meditation and it can become somewhat frustrating. But keep at it and your mind will get better and better at following orders.

In the process you will begin to notice that you are not the brain and your thoughts. You are the observer who escorted the lower mind back to the seed thought over and over again. This is no small revelation and an important step on the road back to the Father. As you dig deeper, focus on this revelation. Who is the observer? The answer in its simplest form is, "You are." The ego will argue that it is the observer, but it is not. The observer is the Self and in that revelation the path of the prodigal son or daughter is clear. You are not your brain and thoughts. You are not the false construct we call the ego.

Tat Tvam Asi. *You are that. That thou art. I am that. I am that I am.*

MEDITATION

Now that you are well on your way to quieting the unruly mind, we move to meditation. This is a state where the mind is mostly quiet, with only a few interruptions during your daily practice. It is at this state that the seed thought focus begins to take on a role in the background while the observer begins to enter into the silence. Ultimately, during contemplation, a step beyond basic meditation, one finds themselves in a state of pure peace. But for now we find that although the mind is occupied with the seed thought, entering the silence is an oscillating process, in and out of the peace. During these moments of pure peace, you know with increasing assurance exactly who you are, the ego has been partially tamed and you are experiencing an increasingly intense recognition of your relationship with the observer. In fact, you sense that you and it are one and the same. This does not mean that the ego has relinquished its claim to royal rank. It still fights for its false status, but it has been greatly tamed by your recognition that it is no longer a necessary aspect of your psyche, and accordingly have removed your gaze from it. In so doing you are starving it of energy.

CONTEMPLATION

Contemplation or samadhi is the natural result of ever intensifying meditation. Pure meditation is contemplation. Once you are there you will know it. In the silence, the secrets behind creation will begin to reveal themselves. These secrets are beyond words or artistic expression to describe, even in symbols, but they are known deep within and the spiritual evolution and path of the One who is the observer begins to be clear to his or her earthly consciousness.

How Long Should One Meditate?

How long should one meditate? It is different for everyone. I will say this. ONE MINUTE OF A QUIET MIND IS MORE BENEFICIAL THAN SEVERAL HOURS OF MEDITATION WITH AN UNDISCIPLINED MIND.

Any length of a quality meditation is beneficial. I like to meditate for 20 minutes in most cases, a few times a day, although as little as 10 minutes is fine if pressed, once you get the hang of it. Now that I am retired, I usually meditate for an hour or so and then write in my journals.

Journaling

What should one write? Well this morning I am writing this piece on meditation. You should write whatever moves you. Sometimes I start writing on one topic and then shift after a few sentences to a totally different thread of ideas. The important thing is to write or otherwise create through art, or sculpture, even problem solving, etc., for it is the best way to bring down from your meditative state that which the earthly realm needs. I believe our creativity comes directly from the higher mind, the place where we can begin to know spirit directly. Creating after meditation opens an ever flowing channel between the higher and the lower planes, and therefor is an extremely important part of the journey, we call life.

How much should one write? Sometimes I write a sentence.

Sometimes I write several pages. I will tell you one thing. Rereading your creative thoughts never gets old. I have journals going back 40 years. Reacquainting myself with what I was thinking back then is fascinating and often enlightening. I am sure you have had, or will have, a similar experience.

And so this completes my thoughts on meditation (at-least for now). Understand, that I have barely scratched the surface. Your own meditation adventure will lead you on a journey beyond description. I look forward to our paths crossing. If you wish to dive deeper, The Yoga Sutras of Patanjali, are at the top of the reading list.

Until then, May God Bless!

CHAPTER 6

A FEW FLASHES OF AWAKENING

*These ideas I like to refer to as **Flashes of Awakening**. In truth all of the numerous epiphanies we encounter on the Pilgrim's Journey are flashes of awakening. They are so clear in meditation, but often elude capture in the 3D world. I also think of them as **Reflections from the Silence**, (The Title of one of my earlier books). They are from the higher mind, touched in meditation and presented here, subject only to the limitations of language.*

- It is far better to give the Love you need and, in so doing, become it, then it is to ask for it and wait.

- I bless what has passed and have faith in whatever may come in the future, as I do my best to express and experience the Father's LOVE in the PRESENT.

- I am a conscious thread within the infinite tapestry of creation. I touch all within the tapestry as all touch me. The tapestry has no beginning and it has no end.

And so we have no beginning and we have no end.

- Spirit is the motivator behind all life. DNA is the template which guides the infinite potential of Spirit into form. Both are of the One Cause.

- The focus of all we say or do must be on the process, or stated another way, firmly within the present moment. If we take care of the present, the results and future will manifest with perfect balance and symmetry.

- Recognize the beautiful gift the body is. See the glory behind it and know it as the earthly temple of your Soul.

- Humility is revealed when the ego gets out of the way.

- Life, physical and spiritual, is an endless process of renewal.

- Open your heart and let all it has to offer the world flow freely. Like the drawing of a warm bath which flows from cold to cool to warm to hot, let your love grow in intensity and consistency.

- Become a witness to your love as it sweeps through the world healing all it touches. Rejoice as it blends with the love of your co-workers, dissolving the illusions of the ego and misguided thought-forms, formed over the millennia.

- Love flows over the world, wherever called, whenever chosen, one encounter at a time.

- Peace is found in the present; Where the Self can be the Self

- The present is a realm of pure peace and wisdom where the Self is free to be the Self, without the constraints of past experiences and related judgements, nor the weight of future expectations.

- Love cannot be hoarded and held unto oneself. Love is energy and must be shared to exist. It must flow to be. Love cannot be given without being returned many times over. But Love given with expectation of return loses much of its power, for it is not really Love. The more one gives of their Love, the more that is returned to them, and the more they know Love. The more one knows Love, the more one knows himself or herself. The more we know ourself, the closer we are to home.

- Let the I become I Am

- Choose to step inside, inviting the Holy Spirit to invigorate you from within, like sacred blood refreshing and energizing one's body, transfiguring through the communion with the One consciousness. The I becomes the I Am as we take a few strides

closer to that which is behind all, to that from which
we came, to that which we have always been.

- Giving paves the way to Love, happiness and peace
  on earth. See all through Loving eyes and rise on the
  shoulders of the Holy Spirit back to the kingdom
  from which we came.

- To have Love within, one must first give it away.

- See all through the eyes of a child, as if you are seeing
  it for the first time, and you will begin to know.

- Love and know no limitation. Only bad choices,
  negative thoughts and holding your fellow man in
  judgement can limit you. These are the choices of
  the ego. They are forged in darkness, but fear not
  for they are dissolved in the light.

- Despair, aloneness and depression are an illusion
  which our own misguided choices have painted in
  front of our eyes.

- Love, give and forgive and your own internal light,
  which is a ray from the One, will reveal the truth
  to you.

- Judgement and feelings of separation from the
  family of man, walls you off from the light.

- Love heals the world by revealing illusion for what it is, Nothing!

- God Bless those who truly Love for they have entered the kingdom of heaven and brought it to earth.

- Awakening is rediscovered in the Silence

- In the silence we reunite with I Am.

- Perfect quiet and balance is the pathway

- Perfect peace is the guide.

- Still the Mind – God is in the Stillness.

- Creativity –

  - It is the creative process or journey that must be pursued, not the result. In true creativity the result takes care of itself. When we create we find ourselves living, acting and being in the eternal NOW. At this frequency we resonate with all potential and all possibilities. Our mind is quiet, our thoughts perfectly clear and precisely formed. We are in control of them and not the other way around. Creativity is the voice in the silence. Hear the voice within, and know that you are it.

CHAPTER 7

SOME THOUGHTS ON LOVE

*E*ach pilgrim has within, a guide, who enables him or her to see the light, interpret it, and bring it into our daily life. We find it within our heart. Its judgement is without flaw. Sadly, we often ignore the wisdom of this inner guide. We look so desperately outside of ourselves for guidance that we easily lose our way.

Turn your gaze inward. There is only one guide. In truth it is our very essence, our true Self, inseparable from the Father Find it and you will never be led astray. The truth is within us. It is written on our hearts but not in words for words cannot express the infinite. It is written in the loving language of His wisdom. Find the perfect discrimination within, and you will know God.

Love is always the way. It is the means, the path and the goal.

LOVE'S SONG

Love cleanses, purifies, heals, inspires, lifts, lightens, leads, quickens, comforts, understands, and carries us to the final destination of the holy evolution some call the journey home. We travel through joyful revelation and growing understanding to pure knowing, sharing, healing and finally, pure being. Always the successful Pilgrim follows the Love Song of the One; the beautiful voice that is forever calling.

We hear the song deep within and like a tuning fork that vibrates in harmony with the vibrations around it, we begin to resonate with its perfect pitch. Soon we become it, as it becomes one with us. We share our good fortune, our gift, our birthright and the song becomes louder and more intensely beautiful, more irresistible. Soon we are joined by others. The song becomes a chorus, each of us adding to its perfect harmonic healing vibratory magic. Our collective song sweeps across creation, both manifest and unmanifest. It heals all that came before, revealing that which was hidden, raising awareness to perfect sight. Each voice adding to the collective oneness, together revealing the keys to the kingdom and pulling back the curtain which has hidden the mysteries for so long.

And so it is. It began with one loving soul hearing God's Love Song, pursuing it at all cost and then sharing it. This is how Love grows. Love shared selflessly soon explodes into His infinite expression.

And so it has always been.

The world is saved one sacred encounter at a time.

God Bless.

BLENDING WITH LOVE

Love is the essence of creation.
Blending with Love and becoming Love is the secret passage through illusion.

Thinking and acting Love, at the beginning of each Pilgrim's journey, is often influenced, without the travelers knowledge, by egoic misdirection.

Conversely, Blending and becoming Love are transcending realizations. They are steps which lift one beyond the confines of the ego and the perceptions of the physical world. Think of blending and becoming, as a drop of water falling into and being absorbed by the boundless ocean. The drop is still the drop, but it is also now one with the ocean. Our individual conscious awareness might be viewed as the drop and the collective consciousness of the cosmos as the ocean. Imagine becoming one with and blending with the collective consciousness. With a surrendering of our egoic ties to the world's illusions of limitation, we enter a greater world, one beyond description, one beyond the ability of the drop to contemplate, yet readily available to the ocean. It all begins with a shift in perception. The good news is that it has always been so. We have just temporarily (out of false fears and illusions) given the ego, our jailer the keys to our cell. Our jailer works overtime to keep us in these cells. It is for our own safety, it repeats over and over. Yes, the lock-down approach to control has been around for eons.

It is time to reclaim the keys and unlock the cell doors of our self- imposed quarantine. The keys are symbols for the awakening to our true self, the process of blending with and becoming Love. 'The truth shall set you free.' The power resides within. It has ever been so. We have only to choose.

CHAPTER 8

The Pilgrim faces many challenges along the way, but there are many more rewards.

More Flashes

The Lie

It seems we can't get through a day without encountering a lie; A lie from our government or someone in power, a lie from false marketing or promotion, a lie from another individual, friend, foe or acquaintance.

What is a lie? Is it a convenient comment uttered to bypass an unwanted confrontation or responsibility? Is it a calculated manipulation tactic by one who needs to control or one who hides something in fear? Is it something the fearful hide behind to avoid the light of scrutiny? The answer is yes; It is all these things and more, but most importantly, the lie is a negative thought-form which grows and festers within the one who has lied. In a very real way it is a small tear in the fabric of our psychic aura, a tear through which our life force is drained and absorbed by dark ones who feed on our energy. This thought form grows with each additional lie until the one who lies, no longer can distinguish truth from lies. Imagine dark entities gathered around the rips in the liar's auric field, sucking and absorbing the sacred energy given to each of us at the beginning of time. Darkness moves into the void which once was your essence. Soon the liar's very existence, his or her life, literally slips into darkness.

The lie continues to fester until one turns to the light and asks to be free of this affliction. It is the surrender to a higher loving power. He or she hears the loving song of those of the light, and through Love's life-line begins the long climb out of darkness. By choosing Love, one is asking for forgiveness and in so doing, asking the healing process to begin. Love and its companion Light, obliterate the darkness, and heals the rips in the etheric shield, the aura.

Choose Love, forgive yourself and ask the Heavens for forgiveness. Know the miracle has unfolded within you. You are again whole. Bask in the light of becoming and continue the flow through unselfish sharing. Most importantly, lie no more for the light knows all secrets, rejoicing with those who have found their way, and weeping for those who are lost.

And so it is.

*When challenges confront us, remember that **I***
* **Am** is just a loving thought away.*

THE CALL AND THE ANSWER

I Am that I Am at this moment
This timeline we know as the present
His Spirit has called and we chose it
To serve in its great presentation
Presenting His glory for all Life
Unfolding the Truth of Creation
His Light does its work of transforming
The form now transfigured, reflecting
The gift of His calling, so precious
His Love through our hearts is exploding
The merging with All now completed
Co-authors with Him our new purpose
By His feet now we are seated
And all of false darkness defeated

Never forget that the Pilgrim's family includes all who walk the path with them. Although no one can walk the path for another, our divine family always stands ready to provide strength, encouragement and protection along the way.

FAMILY SOLIDARITY

The family stands with hearts entwined
With love that bridges heart and mind
True love that seals the family bond
Love so profound, what's lost is found
Freed by faith, their lives begin
Their combined light has cleansed all sin
Uniting, loving, standing tall
Assisting all who trip and fall
Impervious to evil's slings
Which lie and cheat and darkness brings
Repelling all, the family shield,
And sword of justice their light wields
Light conquers dark on battle field
Restoring peace as evil yields
And so the family marches on
Their strength replenished with the dawn
All darkness banished by their light
With restored vision, perfect sight

God's infinite capacity to give is seen clearly in the selfless
service shared freely with us by our mother, the earth. She stands
as a steadfast monument, to all pilgrims, for all that is good,
loving and selfless.

EARTH – OUR HOME

The wonder we call earth our home

Who cares for us and all alone

Sustains our lives so we might share

The magic of God's sacred prayer

With selfless giving, here she serves

Giving more than we deserve

She gives that we might grow and thrive

That we may flourish and survive

The many challenges we face

Her sacrifice we can't replace

For she is selfless, strong and pure

She only cares that we endure

We owe her all, someday we'll know

How much she gave from spring to snow

Upon reflection, it is clear

Without her we would not be here

My heart breaks at what we owe

So many really do not know

Upon awakening, the tears

Fall endlessly for all the years

I was oblivious to all

The gifts that came with her sweet call

And now the time to give has come

To heal the world until we're done

To reach the many and to share

Awakening for those that dare

So bring your light to these few pages

Dispel the darkness of the ages

Join with us in reverie

Together turn the I to We

CHAPTER 9

BEYOND

B eyond all religions, beyond all earthly belief systems rests the truth, the Pilgrim's ultimate salvation. The search for God ultimately leads each of us beyond earthly understanding to pure divine beingness. This is why the quest is compatible with all great religions and loving belief systems (the key word being, loving), each serving as stepping stones along the path home, the path to peaceful transcending truth.

Reclaimed Salvation

We are all conscious threads within the tapestry of creation

Serving the One through the gift of incarnation

Learning to distinguish between effect and causation

Developing wisdom and discrimination

All is drawn to us through Love's gravitation

The world soon is cleansed with each heart's palpitation

Shining His light on false hallucination

Finding the truth while avoiding temptation

Knowing Him deeper with increasing vibration

Each step renews us with Love's validation

Finding true peace through His cosmic oration

A new earth is born through nirvanic gestation

Restoring His plan, healing past inflammation

We are One, becomes our declaration

From darkness to light becomes holy migration

Nothing can compromise His perfect foundation

All heaven rejoices at our reclaimed salvation

CHAPTER 10

With vigilance we take each step.
Always the pilgrim must serve Spirit.

ESCAPE FROM THE DREAM

So many, so long have been led astray
Now they awaken and seek the better way
Those who are blessed must bless others who wake
With the light that they hold for humanity's sake

Awakened to wrongs, by the lies of the dark
And the evil which blinds us from His holy spark
Love's response, never angry, though it seems justified
For our weapon's true love, not fighting false tides

We must be the light that humanity needs
To awaken the sleeping and empower the seed
That was trapped in a dream of hopeless illusion
The result of poor choices, the foes of inclusion

We are light bearers first, One within His great Plan
Knowing Him as the savior of the race we call man
For to maximize life we chose what seemed the least
By serving the smallest, inviting all to the feast

So don't fall for its evil pressing in on your ears
For His Truth sings a song that the faithful can hear
And evil's false promises and all of its lies
Are exposed by the light that you carry inside

CHAPTER 11

PILGRIM MISSTEPS

The answer is simple although so many have forgotten. So many have turned from the glowing light of truth within to pursue shadows of false promises. In time, the glow within is veiled by the haze of illusion and forgetfulness, doubt, separation, despair and ultimately, depression.

In these times we must always remember that the light has not receded into nothingness. Rather it is we who have strayed from its illumination. Our own choices led us into the maze of intellectual rationalizations and its map to nowhere, a map without a compass. Our compass was set aside when we chose our human intellect over the heart.

And so it seems that this is where we are today. Some are living in the glow. Some are awakening from the false dream and the ego's illusion that we are separate and alone, and some are still firmly asleep, lost within the nightmare.

We need to ask ourselves, "Where are we within this continuum of the wandering prodigal son or daughter? Are we lost in the labyrinth of poor decisions and misdirection or have we turned toward the glow and its healing essence which is nothing less than our true self awaiting our return? Are we eating with the swine or have we been reunited with the Father?"

And so the great adventure proceeds. Those who serve Love travel within its perfect glow. Those who serve ego find themselves totally lost in the illusion of the world. Through divine service we fan that glow to the brilliant radiance of its true nature. Know you are an intimate part of the glow and watch as the mysteries of the universe are placed gently into your outstretched hands. Let your heart be your guide. You have only to choose.

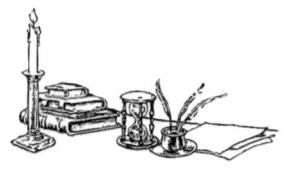

CHAPTER 12

*While in this world the pilgrim is well served by
the constant reminder of who he or she really is.*

ALL HE MADE, THAT THOU ART

ALL HE MADE, THAT thou art
    The Love felt within
    The Joy exploding inside
    The warmth of forgiveness
    That thou art

    The uplifting feeling of giving
    The confidence of knowing
    The sharing of one's Light
    That thou art

    The impulse to serve
    His will on earth
    Communing with the higher

That thou art
Expanding into the infinite
The Love that we share
The Love we receive
That thou art

The Love inside
The wonder of nature
The magic of Life
That thou art

The majesty of the mountains
The power of the ocean
The peace of a still lake
That thou art

The life giving essence in a cup of water
The mystery of the senses
The caress of a soft summer breeze
That thou art

See yourself in all and all in yourself
For that is your true essence
You are that
All He Made, That thou art

CHAPTER 13

CREATION

This poem addresses the concept of creation, the natural attraction of love to itself, the magic of light as consciousness and the reassembling of the sacred hologram, which is creative evolution itself.

> Creating All, through just His dream,
> A thought so perfect, so supreme.
> Pure consciousness soon fills the dark,
> All becomes light with just His spark.
> Comprised of Love, which must attract,
> Small forms begin to interact.
> In time these forms transform to worlds,
> With suns emerging from the swirl.
> Soon life is birthed from Light and Love,
> Sustained by essence from above.
> Expressing perfectly His teaching,

All known within, yet always reaching,

That all can become aware of Him,

He shares His gift, His constant hymn.

Connecting All through Love and Light,

Till darkness fades and all is bright.

Creation is the journey home,

Of consciousness, once all alone.

A journey, never really done,

Until we wake and have become,

The very breath that started All,

Becoming that which is the call.

CHAPTER 14

*This poem, written in 2003, has found its way into some of my earlier
books and is one of my favorites. I include it here because its message
when realized is a major sign post along the Pilgrim's path.*

BOTH FLOWER AND THORN

Have you ever observed on a sunny morn?

How the light embraces both flower and thorn.

How the breeze caresses all with its touch.

Quaking leaves and pine needles everything such,

That none are neglected and all feel His love.

From the least to the greatest, smallest insect to dove.

Mighty rivers and oceans to dew on a leaf.

All are touched with His goodness to the world's great relief.

All encompassed in light, all a part of the whole.

Each an integral player and each with its role.

Only one need be absent and His plan's incomplete.

All must be in the picture before we can meet,

The truth at the beginning where we started our quest.

There it was all along deep inside of our breast.

We were lost in a world that we made with our thoughts.

A world filled with comparing and the pain that it brought.

Where there's better and worse where there's new and there's old.

Where there's black and there's white, where there's lead and there's gold.

He sent light and it brightened all that it touched.

Laying answers before us, a guide giving much.

Quietly waiting for someone to see.

That the truth is a oneness of you and of me.

And the world of comparing disappears in its glow.

For the light has revealed we're all part of His Flow.

Nothing better nor worse, nothing plain nor so fair.

For we're nothing lest He shines within each, to share

Separate bodies we see, separate forms show their face.

But our minds are connected with His holy grace.

So to live life in joy, knowing earth, sky and sea.

Let truth unfold within you so abundantly,

Pain once falsely embraced, never there, now has ceased.

And your heart now knows love and your soul now knows peace.

CHAPTER 15

THE PURPOSE OF LIFE

*M*ost thoughtful people have or are pondering the mystery, "Why are we here and what is the meaning and purpose of life?"

The answer has as many facets as there are pilgrims on the path, but, in my opinion, the common denominator behind all the answers, is Love. Learning to love, mastering its expression, and sharing it freely are the lessons before us. Reawakening to our oneness with it, is the great graduation which opens the gateway to the higher realms.

ALWAYS REMEMBER:

I live to love.

Through love I live.

Loving is the way I grow.

Through growth, I learn to love more effectively.

Loving reveals the truth..

Perceiving the truth frees my soul

A free soul heals the world.

It has always been so.

This is the quest laid before us when time began our journey.

We came into the world loving.

Know this and be a light for those who have lost their way.

Through service, we leave this world as we entered it.

That which we seek is within our grasp.

A pearl of great price.

It is Love….

Love is the glass which never empties

Love is the call from the inner silence

Only love can fill one's life

Love is our very essence.

Unless realized completely, we are less than we can be.

All pursuits are empty without love.

Only love can eliminate fear.

Pledge yourself to the adventure Love has laid before us.

In no other pursuit are courage, wisdom and virtue put more to the test.

In no other pursuit are the rewards more precious.

Through love the path is widened and made straight.

Love is both the challenge and the reward,

Love is both the means and the objective,

Love is both beginning and end.

CHAPTER 16

NEW LIFE

*Nothing is more central to God's creative
principle than the birth of new life.*

A Baby is Born

Through Love, new life presents itself to the world.
It enters on a beam of light from realms which know only purity.
The entering Soul calls for all it needs from the manifested universe,
Which plays its part in providing the building blocks of each soul's
vehicle of expression here on earth.

Guided by His holy template, a human body takes form.
Parents, through their Love, called to the higher realms
And were answered from the illumination of the One.
From the infinite, a single ray, unique, yet one with the whole, heard
the call, and descended.

And through God's magic, a baby soon opens its eyes and
gazes upon its new family.
Love is exchanged as parents and the baby behold each other in the

physical.

Love is reflected in Love and the earthly realm is blessed by this precious gift from above.

Through Love we are granted a peek into the heavenly realms from which we all came.

Remember the love you felt when your eyes first met those of your new baby's eyes, eyes which are windows into heaven.

For, without Love, earthly darkness will try to fill the void

Hold your baby and hear the perfect song of heavens vibration.

The song belongs to all. It is the song which sends all into incarnation.

It is the song which sustains all life and guides those who sense it.

It is the song which calls us back to the Father

And it is the song which welcomes all upon return.

It exists at the threshold between realms

Make it your constant companion

And you will find blessings beyond your greatest imaginings

CHAPTER 17

The greatest growth is always achieved during challenging periods of life. A pilgrims teenage years certainly qualify for the designation, 'challenging.'

A PARENTS SONG FOR THEIR TEENAGER

The angels they brought you, a pearl of great price.
A gift full of promise, a precious new life.
We held you so close, praying never to part.
Your journey in this life, now ready to start.

You're growing, and stretching your wings, set to fly.
Sometimes you fall down but are stronger each try.
We give you our love to help strengthen each day.
As parents, our light's there to help show the way.

So follow you heart, it won't lead you astray
Your mind is its servant, together they play.
The journey commences, adventure awaits.
Your loving intent is the key to all gates.

Our quest is to launch you, not stand in your way.
Our joy leaps within, as you follow Love's Ray
Our hearts are connected, through loving we soar.
These truths they reside within your very core.

We're all on this journey, many paths to one end.
The answer's revealed as you round every bend.
And many are cheering, who have traveled before,
You are never alone as you pass thorough each door.

CHAPTER 18

CROSSING OVER

"Ever has it been that love knows not its own depth
until the hour of separation."

- Kahlil Gibran's, <u>The Prophet</u>

Upon completion of our earthly journey, the time comes to leave the physical world and continue our journey on the subtle planes. These poems celebrate the lives and passing of our family and friends. We will see them all again.

A GOOD MAN MOVES ON

> And so a good man leaves this world
> His sail to heaven now unfurled
> He leaves behind his legacy
> The Love he shared with family
> Pearls left by those who went before
> Have guided him that he might soar
> And find his way to heavens glow
> His karma paid and nothing owed

Free from all debt, his weightless heart

Can hear Loves call for a new start

A life renewed on higher planes

Free from restrictive ball and chains

Though earthly senses see him not

He shares what love and tears have bought

For just a loving thought away

A sincere prayer turns night to day

And so he moves from dusk to dawn

His spotless soul to Love is drawn

A flawless trail he leaves behind

For all who seek the higher Mind

God Bless

A Life Well Lived

She travels free

With the wind and the sea

And the spirit that speaks with its own.

Now unfettered by time,

She rests in the sublime;

Calmly waiting for you and for me.

Look with eyes to above,

There you'll find a white dove

And a glow where the answers are known.

Seek the hand that's outstretched,

Beckoning to the quest

That enables the blind one's to see.

For a life that's well lived,

Find the heart to forgive,

For without it we all go astray.

Innocence that is sweet,

Known in those that we meet,

Will touch all with its heavenly glow.

To a heart that is pure,

Narrow ways become sure,

Touching many along journey's way.

Even those unaware

Find a life of despair

Disappears by the touch of Joy's flow.

So we celebrate life

And its lessons and strife

That we might regain memories lost.

Memories of His realm

And our place on His helm;

Our true home which is free from all fright.

Just a haze since the fall,

But still all hear the call;

We must find it whatever the cost.

Hush the storm that's inside,

Where the false tries to hide

His true wisdom and spirit's insight.

To A Loving Mother

Born to this world with a loving smile, she leaves it as a dove

She travels on with joy to guide, upon a road of Love

A road extended through the years, of life upon this plane

A road built with her joy and tears, and also with her pain

And now upon the golden bridge, to light from up above

She looks behind to those she leaves, with caring eyes of Love

More worried for her husband dear, of nearly 60 years

No one to watch and care for him, is really all she fears

She carries on in crippled form, not caring for her pain

She thinks of others constantly, yet through it there is gain

For God is just, He loves her so, she's held in sweet embrace

And soon she'll rise from earthly weights, a glow upon her face

For years on earth she spread her Joy, and now she takes it with

To blessed realms beyond this world, with wings to travel swift

So patiently He waits for her, until her choice is made

And now this journey's at an end, she goes to Sun from shade

While here she touched so many hearts, so many were her friends

And many lights from up above, await her cross to them

To me a loving mother, and also a true guide

I knew her as a special light, when needed at my side

Her body now is tired, yet in her eyes a glow

She'll soon join the departed, and finally she will know

The truth of this existence, the reason for her life

But those who know her wonder not, a friend, a mother, wife

And so much more she offered, and so much more she gave

To each and all encountered, such love transcends the grave

And now she moves beyond this life, uniting with old friends

Her work continues up above, in realms we'll know again

For death is not an ending, but merely a new start

Continuing our ageless quest, to know God's endless heart

Farewell, our sweet companion, our friend, our lady fair

You travel just before us, upon a path we share

GOODBYE DEAR FRIEND

And so a dear friend moves beyond

What seemed like dusk is now his dawn

A faithful body left behind

What's weak on earth, in heaven strong

He touched so many on his way

So many knew him as a friend

But in the end he could not stay

His future lays beyond the bend

And now he soars, no longer held

By promises made long ago

Remaining contracts, now dispelled

Adventures new, he soon will know

And all around him shines a light

God's gift for all those that he touched

Now even Heaven glows more bright

For secretly, he gave so much

He travels just before us now

For all will follow in their time

Preparing ground with sacred plow

The future promise, so sublime

A new birth we now celebrate

He's in our hearts and never gone

Reunion with old friends can't wait

But we will always hear his song

And so goodbye for now old friend

We send you off with gratitude

The Love you left us never ends

For Love is Heavens holy food

With blessings you are on your way

We celebrate a life well lived

We'll meet again, we hope and pray

Your love you leave as your great gift

We watch your ship sail to the West

The winds push on with steady force

Old friends await the joyful feast

Your captain holds a steady course

We hear the cheers from distant shores

We sense the Love as you arrive

So many waiting by the scores

They say hello, as we goodbye

God Bless

Moving On

Her time here's completed

This life comes to a close

A new journey to Eden

Taking all that she chose

To a new realm of peace

Where forgiveness is granted

Where love will increase

From the seeds that she planted

With new freedom she travels

In a place so sublime

All confusion unraveled

In a realm without time

Timeless peace her companion

Endless freedom's sweet song

Loving Grace, her fine stallion

Racing towards the new dawn

Fare thee well our sweet lady

Fare thee well on your way

Born again like a small babe

Entering a new day

We'll be with you in memories

We'll be with you in prayer

We'll be with you in reverie

When **we** cross here to there

CHAPTER 19

MUSINGS ON VIBRATION

All Creation is vibration. All vibration is life,
From the mineral kingdom to the most sophisticated life forms,
Where there is vibration there is manifestation.
Behind all vibration there is conscious intent.

Behind conscious intent is the One consciousness.
We are part of this consciousness.
We are an indivisible part of the One. All is of the One Soul.
The Soul is the motivator and cause behind All.

We are experiencing consciousness through form;
The form of our magnificent bodies – etheric, physical, emotional and
mental. Gifts from the One Soul. Gifts from ourselves to ourselves.

Within manifestation is the illusion of separateness.

Yet we are an indivisible part of the All.

As we experience manifestation, the All experiences through us,

For we are of it and it is of us.

Through choice our individual and collective experiences are infinite, and so the wisdom of the One Soul is infinite.

Each of us is integral to the unfolding of His perfect plan, reflecting His perfect purpose. Each life dives deep into the density of manifestation, claiming it as God's kingdom.

In time we are all reabsorbed into the One consciousness of which we are forever a part.

And so the cycle continues, perfection beyond perfection evolves throughout the eons, until that which IS, finally rests for a while, and dreams of the next age, perhaps the next big bang.

Each new generation adding to the oscillating rhythm of endless infinite creation, His heartbeat behind All.

And so it is.

And so it continues.

And so it is forever.

CHAPTER 20

This short essay was originally presented in my earlier book, Reflections From The Silence

Musings on Particles and Waves

Science has theorized that all things from the smallest manifestation to the largest structure have both a particle and a wave aspect. The smaller the item, like photon or atom, the more active its wave expression. The larger the item the more active its particle expression. Nevertheless, all things seem to have both aspects expressing themselves to various degrees.

Relating this to the spiritual world, one might say that our everyday earthly existence in our bodies is particle like, separate and individualistic. Whereas a more enlightened expression is more wave like, one with all.

Perhaps the culmination of the pilgrims journey or enlightenment, is the realization of our wavelike nature. When we are expressing our particle nature it is hard to see past our separateness, but when we become wavelike the truth of oneness becomes obvious. Was Christ expressing His wave like nature when he walked on water, healed the sick, or walked through locked doors. Were holy ones who have translocated or levitated also expressing their wave nature. Is the process of merging with our true self a process of merging with our wave expression? This is where science and philosophy merge, where the manifested world and spirituality reveal their common ancestry.

Think about it.

CHAPTER 21

THE CALL OF STILLNESS

Within is a place of pure stillness.
Where movement is barely detected.
Where light is the only vibration.
Potential beyond comprehension.
Beyond all earthly perception.
Sculpting all forms from idea.
Broadcasting templates for all life.
The physical realms of creation.
Yet always residing in silence.
The power beyond revelation.
Calling us home from our service.
Sharing its holy refreshment.
Love flowing through all Light-bearers.
Who soar with each new revelation.

Pure peaceful and holy still waters.

The realm through which all good flows to us.

We only need know and request it.

And soon it infuses our being.

His power, unlimited flowing.

Awakening all with pure knowing.

In stillness it whispers its secrets.

And so we must choose revelation.

Residing so closely in stillness.

The Silence, His gift to creation.

CHAPTER 22

FOOD FOR THOUGHT

Become the Teacher

Love and you teach Love
Be joyful and you teach joy
Understand and you teach understanding
Be compassionate and teach compassion
Let your heart guide and teach the secrets revealed.

You do not need special training
You need only follow your heart

See Yourself in Everything and Everything in Yourself

Bhagavad Gita

We know in others what we have discovered within ourselves. Likewise, the Love we see in others reinforces and strengthens the Love that grows within ourselves. When we realize our kinship and closeness to all life and all that exists, our vision clears and we begin to touch the truth behind the form. It is then that the Holy Spirit makes its presence known and reaches out to us so that, if we choose, we might transcend the body and know the fullness of reality. Love begets Love and is reflected in and through itself. Simple words but infinitely powerful. The truth behind them is waiting to be rediscovered. We have only to choose.

Infinite Consciousness

Take a moment and contemplate the fullness of His infinite creation. Too often we think of man as being at the pinnacle of God's creative prowess, just a few millennia away from Holy Communion with His infinite expression. In some ways this is true but, there is so much more.

What about our beautiful earth? Is it not an entity with conscious intent, and what of the neighboring planets, the solar system, our sun, the stars, constellations, and galaxies? What about the universe or perhaps, multiple universes as many scientists theorize? Are there universes of universes? Is there a collective consciousness, a separate entity at each level of creation, at each ever increasing complexity of united expression. Is there one consciousness which encompass' them all? Is there an end or does the expression of His magnificence go on and on forever; creation within creation, within creation.

So much to wrap our minds around. In truth our earthly minds cannot comprehend it. Only in deep contemplation can we begin to touch its infinite depth. But even the quietest of minds cannot see it clearly, much less bring it back to earth in words, symbols, analogies or metaphor. Yet something deep inside calls us to this subtle reflection of ever greater truths, inviting us to climb the holy stairway of greater understanding. Does it make you feel small, or do you sense something so profound that you explode with inner joy, a joy which cannot wait to plumb the depths of its promise?

Think about it.

CHAPTER 23

A LOVING SIGN POST

And so each year we celebrate another Valentine's day. So much more than a day to exchange cards and candy hearts. Not just an annual opportunity for greeting card companies to meet budget objectives. This is a time to reflect on those we love. This is a time to see Love's power in all, well beyond just families and friends, to an ever growing infinite circle of connectedness. Think deeply on this day of Love. Open your heart and feel its message. Feel its infinite flow and observe where it guides you.

The world wants us to think that Love is saved for only a select few. It urges us to shield our hearts from the fears which it promotes, unknown fears, and yet no less illusionary, unless we choose to let them into our psyche. By living within this illusion, we soon withdraw. We soon exist in a truncated realm and feel increasingly alone. Fear is behind all negativity in the world, all dark thoughts, separatism, anger, aggression, selfishness and ultimately depression and hopelessness.

Valentines Day, as simple and childlike as it may seem, is a ray of light from above, a small remembrance that Love is the way and its message of Oneness a pathway through the illusion. Share your Love, even if only through small acts of kindness and charity, and watch as the light of your Love grows and combines with the Love of others. Give, receive and give again, until the illusion of being separate is revealed for the false premise that it is. It is a simple choice, although at first it seems like a giant and dangerous leap across a deep and ominous chasm.

Look through the lens of your Love, your heart, and the bridge across will be revealed. It beckons all Pilgrims who are lost, to step upon it and rediscover the long forgotten truth of who they really are. Each step is greeted by heavens illuminating light, and the illusion of an uncrossable chasm fades into the nothingness of its founding. Soon a beautiful valley is revealed with its fertile fields, pure lakes and streams, wildlife and glorious vistas. This is our true reality. Valentine's day is a moment in time to reconnect. It has always been so. God's forever promise. We have only to choose. Four simple words, "Won't you be mine?"

WON'T YOU BE MINE

Sweet Valentine
Pure Love Divine
Fragrance sublime
Won't you be mine?

As I am yours
Expression so pure
Beyond allure
Love is the cure

Share Love's bouquet

Along the way

Keep dark at bay

Through Him we pray

And so we share

Sweet Love so fair

Awake and aware

Within sacred air

Not just a date

Love co-creates

Roads become straight

Unlocks all gates

Be Mine – the request

To All addressed

Give first and be blessed

True Love the quest

CHAPTER 24

THE PILGRIM AND THE THRESHOLD

Awakening is rediscovered in the Silence

In the Silence we re-unite consciously with the I Am.

Perfect quiet and balance is the pathway

Perfect peace is our guide to illumination

Traveling without moving we find ourself

In the realm of the One

We see it in our mind's eye

It is just one short step away

But we cannot will ourself to take that last step

No matter how determined

For the final step is only taken by letting go

Surrendering to that which is

Surrendering to I Am

And so we find ourself standing on the threshold

Watching our future dancing in the light beyond

Calling to us, ever calling

Our hearts long to cross the threshold

But some attachment holds us back

Its resonance too low and incompatible with that which calls

And so we remain stranded at the threshold

Pondering the mystery of the crossing

Searching intensely for the keys to the kingdom

Deep inside we hear a voice

A still small voice beyond the pale

We are filled with joy as it's song penetrates deep within

So calming. So peaceful. We are drawn to it.

In the silence it is met with its harmonic twin

The voice, no longer from without, now resonates from within

In the ecstasy of realization we find ourselves beyond the threshold.

In fact there is no threshold

The two have become one

The vast man has reawakened

His kingdom has come, on earth as it is in heaven.

Awakening waits patiently in the silence.

We have only to choose.

CHAPTER 25

SOME THOUGHTS ON DEPRESSION

It is hard to understand depression and its feelings of aloneness, hopelessness and separatism. Those of us with loved ones struggling with this dark illusion often feel helpless in our efforts to penetrate the barriers erected by a depressed mind. Even our most ardent prayers, compassion and understanding seem to barely penetrate a depressed psyche.

Until a depressed person chooses light, progress out of the darkness is delayed. The only way past it is on wings of love; but love is a choice and many who are depressed cannot bring themselves to make this choice, or are blinded by their chosen suffering. Service is the only sure path to fullness. Putting others first leaves little time for depression's false claims of reality. Loving service is God made manifest.

This is something realized and really cannot be taught, although sharing one's light can help remind those who suffer, of the truth inside them. This truth calls one to healing and dissolves the illusion of pain, hopelessness and aloneness. In truth, we are never alone and yet separateness seems so real sometimes. Our bodies and senses attest to separateness, and in our false aloneness fear raises its satanic head demanding to be recognized. But that is an illusion, an illusion which is dissolved in Love's fire. All it takes is a flash of awakening and the natural choice of loving service will present itself to all who begin the journey back to the Father. Our job is to hold the light, know its source is unlimited and that we are all an intimate part of it. With the knowing, it will flow endlessly from the heart flame and heal all it touches. Love does the work. We have only to choose and it is so. We are helpless until we choose. Each of us knows these truths in our hearts. We have only to share our light so that those who call for help from the darkness, can find it, reunite with it and take their place with their brothers and sisters in Light.

CHAPTER 26

TO THE LOST ONES

The pathway home can seem long and treacherous to those who through misguided choices, false guides, or other dark illusions have strayed from God's protective light. The poems below address these unnecessary tragedies. But through forgiveness, service and sharing the light, there is always hope, as the Pilgrim's never ending journey continues.

A Parent's Lament

A Priceless Jewel's lost its way
Joy turns to sorrow, dark the day
So many questions, who's to blame
That we might cast away the pain
And free ourselves from guilt and sadness
We long to know what caused this madness
For we were there to hold him dear
To wipe away his every tear
Dark in the world kept him at bay

We longed for one last chance to say

How much we loved him, how much we cared
We prayed so deep, our love to share
With desperate pleas, we called him near
So deeply lost, he could not hear
Through broken hearts, we sent our love
Hoping to reach him from above
And yet in darkness he had chosen
Decisions made, his heart so frozen
We knocked and pounded on his cage
Imprisoned there in Satan's maze
Nailed upon the Devil's tree
We could not reach him, set him free
We cried and pleaded through our song
He wouldn't hear and now he's gone

In sadness we were turned away
So much undone, so much to say
In deepest love we gave him life
But all he saw was worldly strife
Such darkness, chaos and confusion
Contributing to the world's illusion
And now we seek another trail
Beyond our pain, beyond the pale
A higher calling where we'll find
The truth, somehow we left behind
And in His peace, we'll find again
Our lovely boy, now cleansed of sin
For nothing's final in God's realm
Forever, we can begin again

Forgiveness is the only path
That leads to Him, beyond all wrath
To truth, where all is Light and Love
Where all is healed by the Dove
Must find our Love, reclaim our Joy
For through our Love, we'll find our boy
With arms outstretched, to hold us tight
He knows we never quit the fight
And there in peace, we'll find reward
Within the heart of our true Lord

Sometimes a friend, family member or loved one inexplicably gives up the journey. Here despair and depression have overwhelmed their light. The following poem was written for such a traveler. Our job, as fellow pilgrims, is to hold the light for them until they choose to again pick up the torch and move forward.

TO A FRIEND WHO IS LOST

With heartbreak I watch him, lost in the night
Moving through shadows, just out of sight
Feeling unworthy of His Holy light
Hiding from Love and all that is bright

Some dark false specter now has his ear
Spreading illusions through words of fear
Blinding his senses from all that is dear

Piercing his heart where once was life's cheer

And now false blindness, causes forget

How did such pure love turn to regret

Suddenly, all seems like such a threat

What once was beautiful, now karmic debt

How did this good man fall, lose his way

Watching fear enter, colors turn grey

False guides befriended, and soon lead astray

False guides that he will, soon need to slay

Deep within his heart, the truth resides

Good must awaken from deep inside

Awaiting his choice and the turn of the tide

Waiting for him to awake and decide

To remember his gifts which so freely he shared

So many healed, by just knowing he cared

He gave so freely, nothing was spared

The world so much brighter, 'cause he chose to dare

Somehow he's forgotten his many gifts

So many in need, who he tried to lift

In his forgetting, his faith set adrift

Light became dark and thoughts seemed to shift

How did his joy turn to darkest night

Unworthy perceptions, feeding the blight

Veiling the truth in illusions false fright

The cure so simple, just accept His Light

For we are of Oneness, and never alone
Though all that's evil, wants this fact unknown
Through fears of aloneness, its lies are sewn
Yet it only takes one small flame to lead home

From smallest spark to greatest blaze
God's light can straighten the twisted maze
And clear away the blindman's blank gaze
Purifying his mind of devilish haze

If only he knew how much he's admired
Remembering truth is all that's required
So many he touched, so many inspired
Such gifts return and will never expire

Giving's the key to one's joy on this plane
It lifts one to light, where falsehoods are slain
Such actions and thoughts soon unshackle our chains
And lead us to peace and His holy reign

These words of support, I launch in time-space
That he might remember his work still awaits
Our lives are a marathon, not a short race
For we are light beings, filled with God's grace

CHAPTER 27

A TOUGH LETTER OF LOVE

*S*ometimes the pilgrim walking Love's path must dig deep inside and confront another traveler who has gone astray. No one likes confrontation, especially when the one being confronted is a friend or family member. In these circumstances we must remember that we are all called upon to be light bearers and those choosing darkness are infecting all that they come in contact with. In situations like this we must each find our inner strength and present the truth in a direct but loving manner. Once presented, the truth will do the remaining work. Do not be discouraged if healing seems to stall. Truth's magic works throughout eternity and although you may need to distance yourself from the darkness, today, you may have saved a soul in a future time line.

The following excerpts are from a letter written to one who wanders.

A LETTER TO ONE WHO WANDERS
FROM ONE WHO CARES.

Dear _____,

I write this letter because I can't sit idly by while you slide down the slippery slope to ever increasing darkness, aloneness and ultimately regret. A few weeks ago you were firmly on the path of light and the happiness it brings to you and all you touch. You were saved in baptism and confirmed your intent to live in and share the light. What happened?

What happened to cause you to invite some old friends back into your life. "Which old friends," you ask. Drugs, alcohol, doubt, anger, and the darkness that accompanies them where ever you go. You have a family that cares about you and yet when you come home after communing with these false friends, you bring your darkness with you. It spreads throughout the house doing its best to sweep the joy of a loving family right out the back door. There is no place for darkness in a family, in a loving home. Everyone is affected. The man or woman of the house is there to protect and nurture. He or she is a beacon of light which sends the message of love and light into the void telling all that this is a house of the one true loving source of all, whatever name one gives it. Darkness will not come near such a house, unless invited in by one who has lost his or her way. When even one member of the household abdicates his or her responsibilities, the family weakens and unless that cancer is removed, eventually collapses. Once inside the home, negative energy tries to infect all in the family with weaknesses, that it can attach to. It pretends to be a friend and yet it has only one objective. That objective is to turn light into darkness. Their ultimate prize, YOUR SOUL! The dark ones do this through trickery and deception. They do everything they can to convince you that it is someone else's fault. "Certainly it is not your fault," they say. It is the classic interaction of Smeagol and Gollum (Lord of the Rings).

How do they trick you into stepping off the path in the first place? They do it by finding the weak link. Perhaps you have a friend that is having troubles at home with his marriage or finances. Darkness convinces you to support your friend and suggests a liquor establishment of some sort, at lunch or after work. Your basic goodness convinces you to go and have a few drinks with him. What could it hurt? The bar is full of people who are there for similar reasons, usually a strong feeling of separateness , aloneness, helplessness, a feeling of failure, etc., the list goes on and on. You go home, slightly inebriated and those who love you, sensing something's wrong, confront you. In your numb state you get angry. "How can you question me? I was helping a friend. I work so hard for all of you etc., etc." You have stepped off the path and don't even know it.

Not only are you off the path, but your self-righteousness has placed you firmly on the slippery slope to ever increasing darkness. Again, it is always someone else's fault. You withdraw to the false safety of your own selfishness, and don't even realize that you are now accelerating down the never-ending slippery slope. **Your family begins to turn from you. Not because they don't love you, but because your selfishness has left them nothing that they can connect with.**

If you continue on this path, you will lose everything. There is no place for a selfish ego within a family doing its best to walk the narrow path. Each of us has to tread his or her own path to His sacred feet. Darkness is a significant stumbling block. Reluctantly, the dark one, ultimately, will be asked to leave the family.

And all because of poor choices and a selfish (it's some else's fault) attitude, keeping you from accepting the truth of the situation, asking for forgiveness (which will always be given) and then doing your best to make the right choices and begin to heal the damage done. This is not daunting. You make your choices one at a time. You do your best. Daily you remember that you are the image and likeness of God himself. You are His ambassador in the world. Slowly you become ever stronger in your faith and take your place once again as a light bearer in the world.

WHAT ARE THE STEPS TO SALVATION?

- Accept the truth of your weakness and need for God's light in everything you do, think, or say.
- Ask for forgiveness
- Start making better choices.

    ◦ "But I am to weak, " you say. Yes, we all are, by ourselves, but God never meant for you to be alone. Choose him. Let His strength flow into you and know you have the power of the cosmos behind you and, more importantly, within you.

- Support your family. **Put them first and yourself last.** In this way you invoke the miracle and mystery, that by 'becoming the least you become the greatest.'

- Support them with your fatherhood or motherhood, spirit and treasure. In this way you are creating treasures in heaven. You and your family will thrive and your children will grow strong and true.

- Kick all the false friends (seen and unseen) that have led you astray out of your life and psyche. Avoid alcohol, drugs etc. They are not your friends and will only lurk in the shadows waiting to lead you astray once again.

- And let honesty be your way. Lies are known by the entire heavenly host. Lies veil the light of heaven and are always revealed eventually in the light of the truth.

- Think of your life as an opportunity to serve Him. Let His love and strength flow through you and out into the world. In this way you bring His kingdom to earth every second of every day.

These things I share with you as a loved friend. We owe it to you to help you get back on the path. You owe it to us to try.

God Bless You,

_____

CHAPTER 28

SERVICE

*A*lways and forever the answer to finding one's inner joy is service
to others; Service given freely, without any expectation of return,
service to the light.

SHARING ONE'S LIGHT

Some are hiding themselves from the light of their dawn.

Hiding their unique beauty, fearing judgement and scorn,

From the sleepers who wander in their world of illusion,

Fearing light that might waken, from their endless confusion.

Hiding their true expression from the light that reveals,

The joy of Love's nature, hiding behind fear's shield.

Status Quo is their safety, never venturing beyond.

Hiding in self-made prisons, never gifting their sound,

To a world that is starving for the beauty they hold.

Leaving gaps in creation, leaving stories untold.

Which can only be filled by their love freely shared.

Receiving through giving, these must always be paired.

And the great revelation, His gift and His promise,

Deep within it has waited, for the conscious to notice.

And the picture's revealed so that all soon may know,

That the truth is a Oneness, connecting all in His flow.

Freely shared through the eons, yet beyond time and space.

So with courage rejoice, share the light of His Face.

For your gift heals the world. Fight through all ridicule.

Such a gift is beyond price. Giving , His perfect rule.

Service wrapped in his Love, nothing on earth compares.

For the law of the heavens, starts with Love that is shared.

And receiving will follow, it is the only way.

Embrace truth and awaken, see the night turn to day.

CHAPTER 29

TO THOSE THAT
WILL LOVE US FOREVER

Where would most of us be without those that love or loved us. In most cases these are our parents and grandparents, but not always. This section gives special thanks to those that love and loved us where ever they might be.

To The Mothers

Sweet Mother Goddess, pure in heart
You loved us since before the start
You loved us as we learned to fly
We never thought we'd say good by

Always there to catch our fall
To help us conquer any wall

Until we could stand on our own
Until the time came to leave home
And so we journey down the road
You showed the way. You lightened the load
Our time together went so fast
What once was future, now is past

With endless love, yet heavy heart
You watch as precious ones depart
A part of you is always there
There is no weight you cannot bear

A part of you we'll always be
You love us now and endlessly
Always there to help us grow
We feel you close, but do not know

The true depth of the love you hold
A love that never can grow cold
A love that nurtures, lifts and holds
Soft and gentle, yet so bold

You're like a soft still lake at dawn
Yet tempests flare when there's a wrong
For you are beauty, goodness, truth
You're the foundation, walls and roof

Protecting and enriching all
Supporting family, standing tall
Until we could stand on our own

Expressing love as we were shown

As husbands, wives, as parents, friends
The cycle turns, but never ends
And all the love, our mothers shared
We draw upon, we are prepared

To carry the torch a few more laps
With loving grace, until perhaps
One day we know our mother's love
So pure and flowing from above

Into our hearts for us to share
Connecting all hearts everywhere
And from above, our mothers know
They shared God's love, maintained the flow

Throughout all history and time
Through mother's love, we touch divine.

A FATHER'S STRENGTH

With silent strength, his love's expressed

Most visible in times of stress

But always there to comfort and guide

His family, his joy, his love and his pride

A pillar, rock and corner stone

A love that shows we're not alone

To serve his family is his way

To catch the falling, come what may

He's there to help with heavy load

He sees the vision and the road

He's there to help each make their way

Protect the lost, and guide the stray

His compass is the sacred word

The joy of service his reward

Always there to help and serve

To smooth our path make straight the curves

He teaches, till we are adept

He shows the way, he cheers each step

Though we must travel on our own

He shares his light till we are grown

He asks for nothing in return

He shares the joy as children learn

And so he stands there like a rock

With loving heart, he tends his flock

Never will he step away

His duty clear like light of day

And so he's there through our long climb

And will be loved beyond all time

CHAPTER 30

SOME MUSINGS ON TIME

This essay, like its partner, "The Sacred Hologram," (included above) was written decades ago. Parts of it were included in my book, Water Wisdom, Part 1 – A Journey of Discovery. I include it here because time is the playground the Pilgrim travels through and an understanding of this provides a perspective (IMO) required for the journey.

And so we begin -

Although often taken for granted, time is an essential element of manifested creation. In our world of constant action, it measures the gaps between and during activities. As long as there is action, there is time. We measure days by the rotation of the earth, months by the cycles of the moon, years by the earth's orbit of the sun. We have atomic clocks, which measure the vibrations of the atom and relate these vibrations to seconds, minutes, and hours. If one thinks about it, time is nothing more than the measurement of movement and movement must always be the relation of one body to another, from the moon's orbit of the earth to the vibrations of a subatomic particle.

It would appear, therefore, that time requires movement to exist. Movement manifests as linear, rotational, and vibrational. Some think that light in all its manifestations is the ultimate movement, a constant against which all else in the incarnated world is measured. This is true up to a point. But perhaps there is something before light, before electromagnetism, even before gravity. That something is their ultimate cause. That cause would have to create all that exists and govern their position, movement and relation to one another. I would submit that this ultimate cause is the One consciousness, which unfortunately words fall short of describing.

But between consciousness and creation there are several other variables about which words, analogy, symbolism and metaphor can begin to describe in a unified, coherent manner. Open your mind and consider the possibility that there is a field that connects everything in an intimate, related, and instantaneous way. Some have named this field the ether, source field, torsion field, etc. Some even think gravity is the prime mover. There are many ways to describe it, but if you can grasp the concept of interconnectedness of all that exists, you are well on your way to taking important new steps on the road to spiritual evolution.

Some think the flow of gravity is the cause behind time, but for our purposes, it is enough to relate flow and movement to time, notwithstanding the name others choose to give it.

So, we have theorized that consciousness is behind this flow of charge, and this flow through and around everything together with consciousness, is the prime mover behind creation, which we might also refer to as space-time. Perhaps an atom is merely a vibrational vortex within this flow. The action of the two upon each other might be the cause behind electromagnetism, and the strong and weak force. Perhaps flow when viewed this way provides the essence of the unified force, the holy grail of physics.

Of course these are my musings and have not been vetted with the scientific community. I am merely proposing another way to look at things. Perhaps viewing science from a different angle will trigger some fresh epiphanies by one or more of the worlds brilliant minds. Whether I am right or wrong, what is important is an opening and stretching of the mind.

What we need to see, is the intimate connection of all to all simultaneously, such that the movement of one impacts the whole in a comprehensive, direct, and also mysterious way. Quantum entanglement comes to mind.

Once we can see the intimate connection of all, we need to know our place therein, a place not limited by space or time, but an intimate part of consciousness itself, the cause behind all.

One might think of the flow of charge as the thread from which the fabric of all that exists is woven, directed by the universal mind. Together order is brought to chaos, if you will.

Throughout the ages our sacred scriptures have supported the existence of an initiating cause, a prime mover. 'Let there be light,' and 'He breathed upon the waters,' are both preludes to creation in the Bible. Similar acts of genesis can be found in most creation stories. But what 'breathed upon the waters,' what was the breath, and what called forth the light?

I would submit that consciousness breathed upon the waters, its breath was the flow we just defined, and the waters are the same as the ether or fields, also just hypothesized.

Without creation there is no time, so cause must exist before time in timelessness. That which is eternal is before time or timeless. The soul is eternal, and so it must also exist in timelessness. But the soul also exists through ensoulment in the created world. Perhaps it is our job in life to connect the two, to bring heaven to earth, to bring His kingdom to 'earth as it is in heaven." Sound familiar?

But how does one make this connection? How does one reconnect the soul incarnate to its higher self? Are meditation, prayer, and contemplation the only way?

Clearly they are proven and safe approaches. It is the way recommended and used by all the great spiritual ones who were able to reconnect the lower to the higher. But the universe itself is also currently aiding the world.

Here I am referring to the possibility that our solar system passes through a more energetic part of the galaxy periodically and is in fact doing so now. This might explain the bursts of life showing up periodically in the fossil records. A slight but measurable increase in planetary temperatures throughout the solar system as measured by some scientists also reflects this increased energy. As earth passes through this energy, for the next few generations, humanity will experience a quickening and begin to awaken from its long slumber. We are seeing it already.

The cause is beyond time, as is our true nature. When we pray, meditate, or contemplate, we can begin to touch this state, a state of mind beyond time. Meditation is a quieting of the mind, finding peace, and holding the power of consciousness in a powerful focus. Those who have achieved success in meditation say that time stops, all thoughts cease, and peace is experienced as the meditator merges with pure consciousness, our true state. If we quiet our minds, we are rewarded with the revelation of reality, a reconnecting with our true self.

Since time stops with the quieting of your thoughts, is time a thought? Thought is movement of the mind and thus a realm in which time must exist. We have already seen that to transcend time we must stop all movement, in this case thought, and we must transcend time to touch the prime cause, our true home, the home of the Father and the beginning and end of the journey of the prodigal son.

CHAPTER 31

EXCERPTS FROM LETTERS TO A LOVED ONE DURING RECOVERY

All of us are confronted daily by vast temptations. The gauntlet of life is full of challenges and can only be successfully navigated by one clothed in the armor of Light and Love. What follows are excerpts from letters written to a family member who strayed. I include them because they address many of the challenges each Pilgrim, each prodigal son and daughter might encounter on their journey home.

LETTER 1

.......Yesterday was both a sad day and an incredibly joyful day. Sad because I knew you were frightened and a little unsure of yourself, but joyful because you were on the road to recovery with healing just around the corner.

Sure you presented some challenges, but that is part of life and we have all grown and are better because of it. It's like the serpent and the shedding of its skin. It hurts at the time but once shed the serpent has a new and more flexible skin to continue its growth. Just so, you are in the last throws of shedding a skin which temporarily had trapped you. Throwing it off takes courage and can be a little frightening but there is nothing to really be afraid of. It is just God pushing you ahead. He needs you to join his army. There is much to do. All he asks is that you let Him flow through you and guide your actions and thoughts. Upon accepting this, His energy revitalizes you and you experience joy and love with an intensity beyond description.

Just close your eyes and say to Him;

"Lord I surrender to you, flow through me and guide my actions. I am a candle blowing in the wind without you, directionless like a ship without a rudder. But you strengthen me, straighten the path before me and remove all stumbling blocks. You are everything and I am, an integral part of you when you flow through me. Yet I am empty without you. Take your place within me, and let your light brighten all the dark shadows that have plagued me. Help me to know that they are nothing, have always been nothing and that I have lived in a great illusion, an illusion of my own making. But now the darkness is gone. There is only your unlimited light. The black hole which I once perceived now glows as the brightest star. It is you. It guides me, and I will never lose you again. Thank you Father, for I now know that you never left me. In fact you can never leave me for all that I am is you. If you are everything and infinite how can I be separate from you unless in my illusion I choose to be. Oh Father, with each small revelation of my relationship to you I feel joy course through me lifting me up and healing me so completely that I will never lose you again. You have always been there. How could I have been so blind? Thank you Lord for restoring my sight. I will never leave you again. I love you and now know that my love is you flowing through me. I thought I was alone but the Love I have is you. By choosing Love I choose you. It is so simple. Father I rededicate

my life to you. I am your loving servant. God bless all my loved ones, from whom I am never separate for I love them and they love me. You are Love and infinite. Through You we are never divided but rather a part of the One, a part of your body. I love you Father. Thank you for saving me. Amen.".......

Letter 2

..........There is no mystery to finding God. You are his child. He forgives you the moment you turn to him. You have only to ask, but you must also forgive yourself. If the Father forgives you, can you do anything less?

Healing takes place on a spiritual level immediately upon asking God for healing and forgiving yourself and those who need your forgiveness. Now you have only to heal the body by sticking to your regimen and intensifying your relationship with God. As you do, you will find your Holy relationship intensifying each day. You will soon realize that you are an inseparable part of the Holy body, a part that God loves unconditionally, without interruption and forever.

We create our own worlds by our perceptions. If we think that the world is dark, then our world is dark; If you see beauty, than our world is beautiful. The world is always the world, just the way God created it, but He has given us the choice of how to perceive it and in so doing we choose our life.......

Letter 3

......I often think that the world is a giant university. We arrive with a soul, body and intellect and the ability to choose. The challenge is to choose wisely. We are born with His Word emblazoned on our heart. Those who lead with the heart will know his wisdom and create a life of beauty and abundance. The temptation however, is to follow the mind's directives and this is when we get in trouble.

It is the brain that compares everything, good/bad, large/small, beautiful/ugly, rich/ poor etc. The brain, or lower mind, can only make comparisons and yet the world relies on it for everything. It is a wonderful instrument, but it was designed to be the servant of the heart and not the other way around. If you look at the world you can easily see the mess our brains have gotten us into. This is where we get in trouble and this is why God must be an integral part of one's life and psyche in order for us to successfully navigate the world's twists and turns and know happiness and heaven on earth. Yes, there is heaven on earth. The Heart knows this. The mind can only know heaven through the heart. This is why my charge to "Lead through the heart" is more than a cute phrase.

Think about it. When are you truly happy? For me it is when I am aware of Love in everything and act accordingly. I am never happy when I snap at someone. And why do I snap at someone unless I feel they have slighted me in some way. And why do I feel slighted except that my brain has concluded (through its infinite ability to make comparisons) that someone was not being fair. And why was someone not being fair except that they too have relied on the brain to guide them instead of the heart.

It goes on and on. With the brain in charge, there can be Hell on earth. With the heart in charge there is Heaven on earth. We have all experienced it. We just seem to fall back into our habits of relying totally on the brain and soon forget what it was that really made us happy. This is the lesson that we all must learn in the university called the world. I think that this is why we are here. Those that learn it go on to loftier realms. Those who don't, return here life after life (or if you prefer, continue on in other existences) until they too learn the truth and more importantly put it into practice.

In the Bhagavad-Gita it says to, "Make every act an offering to Me, every thought a gift to Me." All that you do should be dedicated to God, from eating to showering, from conversing to taking a walk. It all starts with leading with the heart. Don't let the mind derail you in your efforts to learn what God wants you to learn while on earth. Remember that you work for Him in everything that you do, and know that those who really keep to this practice are rewarded beyond worldly riches. Wherever you are let your heart lead. Get to know it and you will know joy in everything you do, and all those around you will feel your energy and benefit from it. You don't even have to consciously give it for it to be shared with those who are worthy. For it is its very nature to be shared. What is Love if not shared? Think about it, love not shared is nothing. Love shared is everything. God needs you. You are a part of Him. He needs workers and waits with open embrace for your decision.

It is difficult to put these things in writing for they are lofty concepts which live in the heart and are beyond words. But I know that if you close your eyes and feel your heart you will soon experience their deeper essence. You will find that the road before you will become smooth and life will unfold, no matter where you are, in ways never dreamed of before.

God loves you and is always right there next to you cheering you in your successes and carrying you when you stumble. Love knows no boundaries, it is not limited by time or space, it is infinite and all...........

LETTER 4

..........I just read your most recent letter in which you discuss surrendering to God. It gives me shivers just thinking about it. True surrender is the total answer to a happy and fulfilled life. There is no other way, although we all spend too much time looking in all the wrong places. Most people never realize this or if they do they continue to let their head lead instead of their heart. Unless one surrenders totally by putting his/her heart first, which is putting God first, they haven't really surrendered. You and I have talked about this many times before. Believe me all of heaven rejoices when one of their own comes home. Surrendering completely is coming home.

Controlling your own life and having the confidence to deal with anything that comes along is really what you have been searching for. You've found the answer. The answer is God. The depth that a relationship with God can be plumbed is unlimited. As a servant of the Father, the challenges you encounter will never be faced alone. When you put God first you will know his joy in everything. As you learn to quiet your mind you will be rewarded with infinite peace (a state which we are told is so profound that no earthly experience can come close to describing it). Always you will live within His light. These aren't just words. These things are well within your reach. God wants you to have them.

In one of your letters you mentioned that you wake up every morning happy. That happiness is Him. The love you feel is Him. The joy you feel is Him. God gave us a perfect vehicle (our bodies) to know him. Drugs, alcohol, excessive amounts of sugar and fatty foods, lack of exercise, weird media; all these things desensitize us to his presence. A pure life, fruits and vegetables, exercise, prayer;

these things tune our receptors until you know God's presence like you know your own face in a mirror.......

LETTER 5

..........One of the recurring themes which you have referred to in your letters and conversations is learning to control your anger. If you will bear with me I have some thoughts I wanted to share with you on this subject. The three pitfalls that all great spiritual achievers have had to overcome were anger, fear and excessive sensual cravings. Anger in my opinion is the direct result of attachment. Whether the attachment be to the ego or material things, any perceived or expected loss leads to anger. You can see that anger and fear go hand in hand. Why be angry unless you fear the loss of something which you are attached to. The loss of things, an attack on how we perceive ourselves, a perceived loss of status or spot in the pecking order; and how we want others to see us are all players in this ongoing drama. Yet each of these players requires a reference to the past or the future. Can anger exist in the present moment? If you analyze it the answer is no. Sure we might think we are angry right now, right here, but it is because we are judging ourselves from the past and projecting it on to the future. When we do this we are not living in the present moment, we are living in the past and future. If you really think about it, neither anger nor fear can exist in the present moment. Fear relates to the apprehension of the future so how can it be a part of the present. God is in the present, He is only in the present, so we can only be with Him in the present. When we truly live in the present there is no place for anger or fear. At first it seems hard to live in the present. Clearly we need to plan for the future based upon what we have learned from the past, and this is ok, but once you have set a course, experience it in the present.

Remember when you were a kid and doing something so consuming (working with horses for example) that time flew by and you didn't want it to end. Those moments were full of joy and accomplishment but existed totally in the present. A marathon runner may race on a course that is laid out before him/her, but he/she can only accomplish it one step at a time no matter how gifted. If the runner looks to the end it seems to never come, but if the runner concentrates on one perfect stride at a time suddenly the race is over.......

LETTER 6

.......Anger and fear take you out of the present. Focusing on doing your best with each present moment leads to great accomplishment and joy. Joy is from God and He resides in the present always and forever. It is easy to bypass anger simply by coming back to the present moment. Since God resides in the present moment, it is full of love. Use love as your life line to find your way back to the present moment if ever you find that you have strayed......

........When you live in the present moment, you live in close proximity to God, you radiate loving energy and positive things start happening. Remember that we can only exist in the present moment. Where we run into trouble is when our minds are in the past or future while our bodies are in the present.

The heart is always in the present moment, but if our focus is within the mind, the heart's song is not heard and we live a chaotic and lost life. Only the heart is unwavering. The heart will never tell you to use drugs. If you get an urge, know that it is from the mind. Unless the thoughts of the mind are orchestrated by the heart they will lead you astray. The mind must be brought under control. It must be tamed so that the Heart's song becomes louder and clearer. Silencing the mind is accomplished by developing and nurturing a healthy body combined with meditation and contemplation. Taking care of the body so that it is a fit place for the soul is accomplished through proper diet, exercise, yoga, massage etc. Meditation is accomplished by consistent patient practice followed by journaling which brings the higher down to the physical plane and in so doing reinforces the experiential process. There are many techniques of meditation but anything that quiets the mind (from saying the rosary or mantra to focusing on a subject or object of interest) is on the right track. The important thing is to not let the mind waver. At first this is difficult, but be patient with yourself. Your mind/ego has been in control for a long time and will not give up its position easily. When you realize your mind has wandered, gently bring it back to the subject you are focusing on. Some people focus entirely on the breath. No matter what you focus on be sure to sit with your back very straight and erect.

Think about it. All your problems have at their root a mind gone wild. This is exacerbated by chemical imbalances etc., but it is still the lower mind which is at the core of humanity's problems. Every great sage and saint has had to first learn to control his/her mind. Are you so different from a saint, except that you are a few paces behind on the path back to God. Turning to God lights the path so that we won't lose our way, but we choose to take each step on the path home. Along the way our lower mind and its false guide, the ego, tries anything and everything it can think of to derail our progress. That is why we must spend each morning getting in touch with our heart center such that it becomes our first point of reference when we are faced with difficult choices or perhaps a potential flash of anger. Once our heart points the way we can use our mind as a tool to accomplish an end. Always remember, however that we must lead with the heart. The mind is forever its servant.

Love is the common denominator in each of these methods, to progress on the path home. Love exists in the heart and in the present moment. They are in many ways one and the same. If you follow your heart you will find yourself in the present moment. If you are in the present moment your actions will radiate loving energy helping not just yourself, but all you pass or come in contact with. In this way you effortlessly give back, erasing negative karma and purifying your aura (psyche or sub-conscience) such that you can radiate ever increasing amounts of love. Remember, Love and God are one and the same. The more love you radiate the closer you are to Him until one day all you are is love. This is the pathway of the saints, a pathway beckoning each of us. We have only to choose.........

Letter 7

........As you heal, we all become a little more complete. We all heal together. You are never alone. We are right there with you. We can't do it for you, but we are there with each step you take, cheering you on and rejoicing in His miracle of Love. You are that miracle. We all are. His unlimited forgiveness and compassion stands ever ready to give us the energy and encouragement we need to continue the journey home.

We all ask the question, "Who am I, how do I learn who I am, and upon learning how do I become myself?" These are questions asked by everyone who searches for meaning to life.

In understanding who you are it is important to recognize the eternal nature of the Soul. You are who you have been since before the beginning of time, an extension of the one who made you, a witness to His infinite nature, created to experience and know His joy, to know Him so completely that ultimately you merge with Him and share all that He is. This is His promise and your birthright. "You are a boundless drop in a boundless ocean" (Khalil Gibran), sent by the Father out into time that you might know Him completely. Sure you have stumbled, we all have. But, each time we get back up we become stronger and better able to serve.

But you ask, "Why didn't God just make us perfect from the beginning; Why do we travel this road of pain and confusion?" One answer to your question is that God gives each of us the power of choice. To climb the highest mountain we must choose to do so. For God to put us on the top does little for the growth of the Soul. Sometimes I think of it this way. God who is omnipotent, infinite and omnipresent sends His rays as sparks (each of us as consciousness) out into the void to establish His kingdom in the emptiness. These sparks can choose to let the Father's light shine through them or they can reject the light. Through the pain of learning, those who rejected the light eventually turn back to the light embracing it and ultimately shining brighter than even those who initially chose light. In this way God penetrates the void, a void that does not exist until God sends His light into it. This is the creative process and a mystery which we cannot fully understand. Why would God who is infinite need to create? Why is it Love's nature to create? The fact that love which is infinite becomes greater through its own creation is a mystery that for now we need only accept. Perhaps someday we will understand…..

LETTER 8

……Life is like climbing a mountain unaided, no ropes, no chocks, pitons or carabineers, only our faith to protect us. All of us slip in life and all of us fall. To achieve and ultimately succeed we have only to pick ourselves up and start climbing again. To do this takes faith, a faith that grows with each success. To grow we have to take risks, risks that might lead to a fall. Faith in God seems like a risk to the head but to the heart it is the strongest rope. Always success begins with picking ourselves up off the ground and beginning again. Sometimes we are frightened of the fall and we hide from our dharma (responsibility), but this only leads to greater pain until we soon conclude that we must start climbing again. This is where you found yourself a few weeks ago. You are in the process of reengaging with life, taking it head on. You have found that spark of faith within you which is urging you on. Success is in the doing. Summiting to a tough climb has its rewards but we have already succeeded if we but climb, picking ourselves up each time we stumble, learning who we are with each fall, over and over and over and over again. Who am I you ask? You are a servant of God created before time began to establish His kingdom wherever you are. Each time you say the Lord's Prayer, you evoke the establishment of His kingdom on earth. "Thy kingdom come, thy will be done on earth as it is in heaven." Think about what makes you, you.

When are you truly joyful? You will probably say, "When camping or experiencing nature's beauty; when helping others;

when immersed in a creative endeavor; when experiencing the freedom of exercise, skiing, hiking, etc., etc., etc. Now if we dig deeper we find that in each of these activities there is a subtle but tangible joy. Peeling the onion further we find that this joy always is accompanied by an open heart, an inclusiveness of all that is seen and unseen. An open heart is a giving heart. It has to be for it is where love resides. Whether you are sharing your love through a euphoric moment (skiing, enjoying nature) or giving of yourself for the benefit of your fellow travelers (creating beautiful artwork to share with the world, tending your garden, cooking a meal) you are experiencing joy which is experiencing the Father directly. The reason that this feels so good, so natural is because you are of the Father. These aren't just words. You are of the Father. When you feel you, you experience the Father and know who you are. You experience who you are by sharing your love. It is that easy. This is how you find yourself; this is how you stay yourself. This is how you choose the Father and serve him. This is how you save someone in need, and ultimately this is how you do your part to save the world. It is natural to give your love and live a selfless life. It is unnatural to be selfish. It is natural to be full of joy. It is unnatural to live in pain. Choose and be free. Choose and be yourself. Choose and take the first step back to the Father.

It is all about giving. There is a secret to proper giving. You give by being an example of His love on earth. You give by never wavering from Christ's example. You give all that is of Him. With each gift He rewards you 1000 fold. By being joyful, you give a gift which transcends all others. By leading with your heart you will know compassion and through an ever developing discriminative faculty you will act accordingly. Give that which is most valuable, that which is permanent, that which transcends the ravages of time.

Give of the light and love which He has given you and you will never lose your way again.

And you have so much love. The pains of your misadventures have carved a huge hole in you, a hole which God stands ready to fill with unlimited love the moment you turn to Him. And you have already chosen Him. I hear it in your voice; I read it in your letters. You are learning to give (without expectation of return) and in giving you have already chosen. Give of His love in all its many forms of joy, compassion, patience, forgiveness, beauty and creativity. Give of your goodness. This is the key to walking the razors edge. If you become lost you have only to Love to find your way. It is a light in a dark place, a light unto the world. Listen and choose through your heart. The mind will then serve the heart and together bridge the gap between heaven and earth. There is no place for selfishness in giving. There is no place for ego in compassion. Find yourself and you will find humility. Follow love with relentless passion and you will find your true self staring back at you. Serve Him and become yourself. Serve Him and become the joy that you truly are. Even during difficult times your joy will carry you. Joy is eternal. You will learn through your meditation, prayer and worship the eternal nature of the Soul, your relationship to God, and your purpose within God's plan. You will not be able to put it into words for words cannot touch such a revelation, but you will find peace and know that you are home......

LETTER 9

........I am sorry that your life took a temporary detour, but in a way am glad that you have those experiences to draw strength from as you continue your journey. You have been presented with experiences that few have, or survive from. The wisdom that you can glean from them will serve you the rest of your life. You are one of the lucky ones. You made it out. You have cleared your mind of the cobwebs and are heading down a path of giving. God has given you a unique opportunity to serve Him. I don't know what form it will take but it will somehow touch many people, people who are lost and need your wisdom and patience to find their way through the fog, a path you have already traveled. The truth is that you are helping thousands just by figuring things out and striving for health. When you focus intensely on something, you create thought forms and in effect leave a trail for others to follow after you. Just keep in mind that all the good energy you generate through your patience, forgiveness and joy goes out into the world to do battle with the darkness of hatred and evil that the ego has gotten us into. This is how you become a soldier of Spirit and do His work on earth. Every good thought and action is a weapon against the fog of ignorance and a shield protecting you and all your loved ones…….

…..There is something magical at work and I can't wait to see how it plays out, one loving moment at a time. I can see such a change. The change is your ever increasing ability to be yourself, to love yourself and share that love with all around you. You may have lost sight of it for a while but now you have found it again and it is beautiful. You have so much to give to the world. Know in your heart that heaven rejoices with each step you take into the light. In a very real way this is the process of enlightenment, a path we must all travel to find our true selves and bring meaning to the world. You are on that path now…….

LETTER 10

....Whether you are aware of it or not, we are all in this together. When you fall, we all crash. When you succeed we all soar on angels wings. It is all about surrender. Surrender is something we all must eventually achieve. You have been given a great gift, for God has given you a life where its circumstances are intensely drawing you towards him. Most so called healthy people never come close to surrender. Yet surrender is the fastest and most direct path to heaven. I pray every day that I might have the strength to totally surrender to God. The truth is that the love I feel for you in your hour of need has brought me closer to God than I would ever have achieved otherwise. In a very real way I feel like you have unconsciously taken one for the team. All of us are growing because of your situation.

We are all together for a reason. There is darkness all around trying to encroach upon our faith. In some mysterious way God is giving us an opportunity to grow ever closer to Him. He is inviting us to be a part of his army that we might bring a little light to the world.

When you think about how love works, how it can only be shared, never held, you begin to realize the beauty of Gods plan for all of us, how perfect it is and how all of our life is the opportunity He gives to us to become one with Him and share in His perfection. That is why I think your life is truly blessed. For mysterious reasons He is giving you an enormously intense opportunity to find heaven on earth. He knows you can do it, otherwise things might be different. I know it sounds strange, but if you subscribe to the theory that all life is given to us to find God, then He must want you badly on His team. Think about it and use it to find strength when your humanness tries to convince you to give up. Use that strength to find your faith and laugh in the face of adversity. Eventually darkness will surrender and you will know peace. There is nothing in this world like real peace. That is where you are heading. It is the pearl of great price, the Holy Grail. Most people don't even realize that this is the reason we are here, to find our way home. Fewer still ever attempt the journey. Count yourself among the blessed ones. Don't ever give up and you have to succeed. All those who try are so much better for it. Your comment to us in a recent letter is so apropos, "the greater the sinner, the greater the saint." The world is full of future Saints battling with darkness. Those who achieve the latter never gave up ......

CHAPTER 32

STILL MORE FLASHES

While contemplating the peace of the early morning, the following verses jumped into my journal.

WHO AM I

I am Love trying to break through the illusion of being alone

I am Oneness fighting for recognition in the physical realm

What is true above is veiled from the senses below

But can never be hidden from the heart

The truth from above enters the world through the heart

Like a dolphin using sonar signals to find its way

So the heart sends out signals of Love, to navigate this world

Through Love the path is revealed

What was hidden by illusion coalesces into its true nature

A nature which was never lost

Rather it was a vibration just beyond the earthly senses

But not beyond the heart

Great ones have told us, "Love is the way"

Let your heart lead and never be lost

Let mind find its role as servant to the heart

Together they reveal God's Kingdom on earth

Heart and mind travel the road together,

The road of awakening to His Kingdom on earth

The Realm of Silence

We search for the Silence. We search for His peace.

A realm so exquisite. That seems out of reach.

It calls and we answer. Our senses alert.

But senses can't touch it. And neither can words.

But somehow we hear it. Somewhere deep within.

Our hearts long to join it. New life to begin.

Our whole body quickens. We leap beyond time.

Traveling without moving. We touch the sublime.

No feeling describes it. No words and no thoughts.

Its presence known only, by the joy that it brought.

Angels sing in thanksgiving. The truth behind light.

We have only to choose it, to invoke Heaven's might.

It has always been with us. Blessing all from the start.

Follow Love and you'll find it, on its throne in your heart.

CHAPTER 33

FINDING ONE'S JOY

Time stands still when joy comes over you. It is a gift from your higher self. Just know that it is your birthright to feel joyful and let it happen. Joy is the subtle energy from above which connects the higher and the lower. We react consciously and subconsciously to this connecting energy. It nourishes us, completes us, and reminds us on all levels that we are One.

Have you ever felt joyful, but when you stopped to wonder why, it departs? I can remember in Jr. High, waking up and feeling full of joy, but upon remembering that it was a school day and I was about to enter into the crucible of Jr. High politics and the insecurities of growing up, my joy disappeared. I used to wonder where my joy had gone. It was years later that I realized we make our own reality by how we perceive the world and our place in it, and that I was responsible for the proliferation of my joy or its assassination. Fortunately we all get through Jr High, but do we all realize our part in creating our reality. Energy flow is impacted by intent. If we choose joy with a faith that it will be so, we can greatly improve our energy flow and related health, creativity, understanding, compassion and general well-being. If enough of us choose joy, we will change the world. A few, like Jesus, have even been able to perform great miracles. Did he accomplish this by manipulating energy with his perfect faith and understanding?

One might ask, "What is joy energy?" Is it a separate energy that we feel when we are happy? Is it our natural reaction to the energy of life, the flow of prana, the Holy Spirit, Chi or Psychic Energy. There is energy all around us, from the light spectrum, both visible and invisible, to vibrating energy particles or perhaps strings which comprise all sub atomic particles and ultimately all of creation. There is also spiritual energy of unimaginable power, yet subtle and known only to those who have found peace, within which it resides. I would submit that we create patterns with our thoughts; patterns which when combined with energy manifest as holograms, ideas or other creation of greater or lesser impact depending on the passion behind the intent. Our intent creates these patterns. We can choose happiness or despair, joy or sadness, hope or hopelessness. How we choose will be reflected in our reality. The passion and duration behind our intent determines the power of our creation. Choosing joy with passion sends a powerful healing wave out into the universe. These waves seek their own and grow until their message becomes irresistible, overwhelming the negative and dark with light and love ,which once started, continues until its job is done and then is returned greatly magnified to the sender. Like a tuning fork it raises the vibratory level of all it comes in contact with.

It seems that certain institutions and power centers want us to live in fear. They stress our differences with other groups, racially, politically, and philosophically. It seems that in the name of tolerance they foment racism by stressing the differences with unending monotonous repetition. We are surrounded with exaggerated fears of various diseases, unseen terrorists, crazies with guns, nuclear disaster, natural disaster, child predators, computer fraud, identity thefts, and the list goes on and on. All of these fears impact how we perceive our reality. When fear is the motivator behind our intent the result is a pattern of separatism, aloneness, despair, and hopelessness. The natural flow of love energy from our spiritual-self is greatly restricted and the wonder that is Man becomes a small pigmy-self of his/her potential.

Love/Joy energy can only flow unimpeded when one recognizes his/her Oneness with all of creation, the Oneness of Consciousness. Fear causes us to withdraw from such lofty revelations, to a separate dark and cold reality. This is why, especially now, our work of manifesting reality through Joyful intent is so critical. It is natural for Man to know his True Self, but the journey requires the energy of Oneness, the energy of Joy, the energy of Love. Those who seek truth need our light, as do those who, from a misguided perception of the world, foment fear.

How does one help? How can one make a difference? It is very easy. Align yourself each morning and evening with Light and Love and then go out into your daily life and heal the world one encounter at a time. Like a pebble thrown into a pond, the ripples from your efforts and intent will grow exponentially. Remember that the light from the smallest candle illuminates the darkest room.

CHAPTER 34

TRANSCENDING PAIN

*T*oo often we find ourselves dwelling on feelings, often painful memories. Observing these thoughts, feelings and ideas without attachment can be a healthy exercise, but dwelling on them with attachment is not.

This morning during meditation, my mind wandered to a particular family related challenge and I found myself totally consumed by the related pain it caused to well up within me. When I eventually noticed that my mind had strayed, I brought it back to the silence and was unexpectedly confronted with the inner question, **"Why do you dwell on pain when, I Am here?"** The poem which follows was the result. Hope you enjoy.

For I Am Here

And so you walk the world's roads
You feel alone with heavy load
The world's unkind, you know each tear
You feel your pain, yet **I Am** here

You've made the choice, you've lost all hope
You do your best to live and cope
You've chosen sadness, embraced fear
You've chosen dark, yet **I Am** here

And so reality is made
From paths we've taken, roles we've played
It seems so natural, seems so clear
You chose illusion, yet **I Am** here

I gave you choice to find your way
Back home to me and yet you stray
With each right choice, hear Heaven's cheer
Sharpen your focus, for **I Am** here

Why dwell on pain when I am Joy
Through loving choice, your pain destroy
Reclaim your legacy, truth so dear
Pure Light and Love, for **I Am** here

Don't dwell on sadness, don't choose pain
Along that path there is no gain
Quiet your mind and you'll soon hear
Come, claim my gift, for **I Am** here

It's up to you to choose your song
The journey's short, you've made it long
Turn towards the Light and I'll appear
Just stay the course for **I Am** here

Make Light and Love your faithful guides
Humility to replace pride
One choice away, you are so near
I offer peace, for **I Am** here

Choose Love and Light and heal the earth
Time to awaken, know rebirth
Awaken all on earthly sphere
Find Heaven on earth, for **I Am** here

CHAPTER 35

A FATHER'S PRAYER FOR A LOST LOVED ONE

*A*ll of us have dealt with the loss of a loved one, either through the natural process of the Soul's journey or an unexpected loss due to an accident, mental instability, or poor choices like substance abuse and inevitable addiction. This poem addresses the latter. Of course, worry and heart break are one's first reaction, but soon we come to the conclusion that all healing comes from the Father, the One love behind all.

My natural impulse, like many fathers, is to fix the problem, rescue the victim from Satan's evil bonds and make all right. But, of course we are all helpless in such endeavors until the wanderer chooses to find healing. God gave us free choice and not even He can intercede unless invited by the one in need of healing. Imagine His deep ache when His children turn from Him. He is omnipotent, and yet powerless to do anything unless asked. I wonder to myself, 'If God is helpless to intercede in such situations, who am I to think I can do more.' It is an interesting lesson we all learn along the way. I am still learning it .

LOST

The pilgrim hides and runs away
So terrified of light of day
In darkness, hidden, come what may
Until the end she plans to stay

She feels alone, she lives in fear
Oblivious to love so near
Eternally, she is so dear
Yet, she has chosen not to hear

Within her father's heart an ache
He prays that somehow she will wake
For endless love is hers to take
One simple choice to stem the break

He sends his love through God to share
That she will feel his heartfelt prayer
He knows release from Satan's snare
Is just a choice to breath fresh air

Forever he'll be there for her
He prays that love will clear the blur
And deep inside the truth will stir
As gentle as a kittens purr

He prays that she will reach her hand
Against all evil, take a stand
Demand her rights, reclaim her land
Forever darkness will be banned

He prays for strength to hold the light
That Satan's darkness they might smite
And cleanse creation of this blight
Restoring perfect loving sight

He prays to God to hear his plea
That she awaken and be free
Cast Satan into fiery sea
And let perfection come to be

An answer comes from God within
I cannot heal lest she begins
By choosing light, that's always been
She'll soon know peace and not the sin

My heart embraces all I made
The light within will never fade
My gift's free choice, I cannot aid
She must choose light and not the shade

Within my heart is her birthplace
But false fears keep her from my grace
In time she'll find her special place
Pure knowing in Love's sweet embrace

CHAPTER 36

A DIALOG WITH PERFECTION

I ask the Lord. "Why do you wait to heal the world? Why do you not respond to the prayers of billions?"

And deep within I hear the answer. "I wait only on you. All I have created is a perfect reflection of the One Principle behind all, a reflection of I Am, a reflection of me, and when you awaken you will know it is also a perfect reflection of you. I have given you freedom of choice. I wait only on you to recognize and choose the truth. Time is your playground and in time all mysteries will be revealed. Choose wisely and time transforms into the present. Awaken to the perfection within and all around you and merge with the blissful infinite nature of all. Choose love and feel the embrace of forgiveness and perfect relationship which is your true essence. Awaken to your oneness and time disappears. It exists only to give you the space needed to reacquaint with your true identity, your true reality. It allows you to grow back into your perfect knowing and existence, from which you came and in truth never left. Your journey is leading you steadily towards a very real awakening. Time is your companion. Merge into the truth of oneness and time disappears. It is however long you make it. It is your choice. Time provides a linear perspective in the physical world to help you find your way, as you experience all the physical world has to offer. Surrender and awaken to the revelation that you are the One, and it is you."

"But," I protest, "I am afraid of losing my individuality."

The voice within answers, "You can never lose your uniqueness, but you are also, never separate. Love is the common denominator that cements all with all. But more profoundly, Love is All. Follow it. Let it grow, Become it and save the world. This is the task before you. Choose wisely and become a light unto the world. It is my gift and your birthright. It is you."

CHAPTER 37

LOVE - OUR LIFE BLOOD

SO WHAT IS LOVE?

It is what we feel when we look into the eyes of our children, witness a kind act or immerse ourselves in nature's beauty.

It is a profound sharing of oneself, a selfless act of giving and forgiving.

It is a deep connectedness with another.
It is a deep connectedness with creation in its many forms and as one.
It is knowing our oneness with the Creator behind all.

It is the life blood behind all, flowing, creating, sustaining and motivating all that is, was or ever shall be.
It is the very blood which flows within us.

It is life endlessly and forever quickening, sustaining, and invigorating.

It is the consciousness behind all, the Will that powers and directs all, flowing through the dimensions of creation, in all directions simultaneously.

Our bodies are exquisite vehicles through which to experience the physical realms, but we are so much more. We are the very life blood of the cosmos, the ether connecting all with itself.

Let go of the anchors of materiality and soar within His life flow, the flow of Love.

Dive into the flow, with full confidence of your place within His all.

Melt into the cooling flow of His essence.

Touch and be touched by all that is, reuniting with the Oneness that is.

Lose the false sense of separateness' while celebrating your uniqueness, a uniqueness presented to you before time began.

We are the blood of life.

This infinite embracing consciousness we call Love, is a flowing infinite ocean. It is power beyond words touching all through infinite expression, and yet always One.

Feel its pulse, merge with the infinite heartbeat. Know it as your own.

Choose Oneness and hear the cheers from the heavenly Host as another Soul is welcomed home.

CHAPTER 38

THE ULTIMATE OBJECTIVE

Two Become One

The gift of life provides the stage

On which we stretch to Light from shade

The endless search to find the Self

To leave behind the pigmy elf

The small one that we think we are,

Soon melts away before the star

We reunite and become whole

With that we lost so long ago

The dual nature of our world

Hides mysteries that we unfold

To know the secrets of our dream

And learn Truth's not what it might seem

We walk the earth as half, not whole

To be complete our only goal

All desires long pursued

Are not the answer we must choose

Duality, the great illusion

The genesis of all confusion

A loving heart unites the two

Which becomes one, true love the glue

Selfish desires soon consumed

All false illusion now is doomed

CHAPTER 39

In many ways "Reach Higher," should be the pilgrim's battle cry. The journey and its challenges may seem long, but the rewards are beyond earthly expression. "Reach Higher" was originally published in my book, Reflections From the Silence.

REACH HIGHER

When life mistreats, you feel alone
When darkness seems to freely roam
Gaze upward and behold your home
Reach Higher

See endless heaven in your heart
The love inside will never part
Emblazoned there, till end, from start
Reach higher

See His perfection in the trees

In birds and flowers, humming bees

The gentle caress of the breeze

Reach higher

For it resides in all you see

In all you hear and touch and feel

In giving and a smiles appeal

Reach higher

It's always there, a part of all

It picks you up from every fall

It stretches you to make you tall

Reach higher

Through endless journey, it is there

Supporting you to help you bear

A gift while climbing heavens stair

Reach higher

For there's no limit to one's growth

No meets and bounds, no castle moat

Turn to the light, sing through God's throat

Reach higher

And soon you'll see with open eyes

And know the secrets of the wise

That which you are, begins to rise

Reach higher

All that you see, reflects this truth

Hidden from the profane, uncouth

The secret of eternal youth

Reach higher

And so now take the lessons learned

From darkness, now to heaven turned

The truth revealed like butter churned

Reach higher

No longer lost, we hold His light

The way back home, revealed bright

The blind have now regained their sight

Reach higher

So now awake, renew the quest

Hearts beat anew within each chest

He only asks we do our best

Reach higher

CHAPTER 40

A FEW CLOSING THOUGHTS

DUALITY

At the root of our human desires lies duality. As our long search for wholeness awakens our higher sensibilities, we pass through the gates of illusion and the two become one. At that moment, duality dissolves in the light of our awakening.

WHOLENESS

The body resides in the realm of duality. The body provides the vehicle through which we experience the physical. Yet, wholeness lies beyond the body. Eventually, when all physical avenues of discovery are exhausted, we turn inward.

Learn all the body has to offer and you will one day find you have moved beyond the body, beyond duality. Know your earthly desires to be a reflection of duality in the physical realm. We long for wholeness, that something missing in the world, something just out of reach. We chase endlessly after worldly treasures, thinking they will surely lead us home, but they cannot give us wholeness. Wholeness is only found within, a world we must all eventually choose to explore. When we do we find our all.

The Continuum

The continuum of all that is, spreads across creation like a vibratory tapestry. At each quantum vibrational level is contained unlimited knowledge and wisdom. To touch and unlock the secrets of each level we must resonate with each vibrational level's signature. Within each level are multiple octaves and related harmonics, but all are frequency and by matching one's frequency with each level we are invited to explore its mysteries. It is a glorious quest. Just as we now vibrate in third density and are exploring and resonating with the secrets of the physical world, so we will ascend back to the Father on this endless loving staircase which moves through all levels of creation. At each level we are reacquainted with our true self on that level until we have fully absorbed the gifts offered. These gifts have always been ours. We merely left them behind as we plumbed the depths of involution, or the exploration of ever greater density. Now we travel back up the golden stair reclaiming that which was left behind, reuniting with each level as we climb home. This is the spiritual evolution back to the Father. This involution and evolutionary quest was chosen by each of us at the beginning of time. It is the story of the prodigal sons and daughters returning home.

In the process of reuniting we rediscover, understand and heal that part of the tapestry uniquely ours.

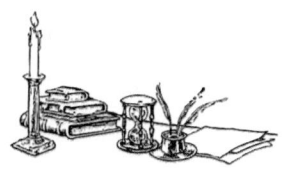

CHAPTER 41

A POEM IN CLOSING

*A*nd so we come to the end of this small book, but certainly not to the end of the glorious journey. I thank you for joining with me on our mutual quest. I have tried to share the energy of the flashes and reflections which have blessed my quiet moments. However, I am well aware that I have fallen short at transmitting their beauty and mystery. Nevertheless, it is a start. Seeds have been planted and plants already growing have received some much needed water. It is my hope that the reader hears within these chapters, however faintly, the music which compelled me to write them. If you have made it this far, you most certainly have; and I am sure you have so much more to add beyond what is shared herein. With deep appreciation, I welcome you as fellow travelers, Pilgrims on our heavenly journey home.

SPIRIT'S CALL
OUR DIVINE PARTNERSHIP

Quiet the mind that I might flow
Become a witness that I might grow
And love will cleanse you, white as snow
With healing light, that all may know

I hear your pleadings in the dark
To share with all, what's in your heart
Guided by light from holy spark
Together a new world we will chart

I sent you out that you might learn
And through your choices, you might earn
And gather wisdom at each turn
And through loves flame, all darkness burn

And in its place pure revelation
Your view now clear from elevation
With clarity and exaltation
Beyond effect, you know causation

Just take my hand, your load I'll lighten
Where there is darkness, I will brighten
No more can evil fool and frighten
I'll lift your hearts, and wisdom heighten

And all now lost, our love will heal
With deep compassion now you feel
We'll cut their bonds with sharpest steel
And free them from their karmic wheel

And light will conquer all illusion
No more wandering in confusion
For all are cleansed with Love's transfusion
No longer hiding in seclusion

One simple choice declares the light
Beyond all doubt with perfect sight
Dark stands aside before our might
You serve the One as Holy Knights

You travel on, but not alone
 Have faith, your love will lead you home
With compass true, all answers known
And with each step your sins atone

Rest in my peace, My Love you know
Safe from false dangers from below
My truth I give that you might sew
Through loving action seeds that grow

The first step now is up to you
Together we will make all new
And bless the world with Spirit's dew
Our mission holy, just and true

Within my light there is no fear
My light reveals and makes all clear
So you might climb tall cliffs, so sheer
And find your way to heaven's cheers

The trail you leave, the path divine
Calls out to all in song sublime
You are the grapes, I am, the vine
Our love ferments to finest wine

EPILOGUE

And so this portion of the Pilgrim's Journey comes to an end; of course, there are no ends, only new beginnings. With each step home the terrain will become increasingly familiar, for we have traversed these paths before. Soon we will rediscover the sacred and intimate relationship between the individual and the Absolute. Growth is eternal. Consciousness is without end.

See you somewhere on the road ahead.

God Bless

www.ingramcontent.com/pod-product-compliance
Lightning Source LLC
Chambersburg PA
CBHW051225210726
48290CB00003B/810